The Greatest of These

The Greatest of These

One Family's Struggle during the 1930's Great Depression

Hi Lavierre + Don,
Thanks for supporting my dream, and happy reading. I hope you enjoy this as much as the great feedback I've had. A page turner they say. When in

Dorothy M. Foss

Duluth, hope we can get together.
Love
Dorothy

Library of Congress Control Number:		2011913575
ISBN:	Hardcover	978-1-4653-4555-4
	Softcover	978-1-4653-4554-7
	Ebook	978-1-4653-4556-1

This book was printed in the United States of America.

To order additional copies of this book, contact:
Xlibris Corporation
1-888-795-4274
www.Xlibris.com
Orders@Xlibris.com
97300

Contents

I dedicate this first novel to my daughter, Pam Forbes, who herself worked as a writer in a corporate Marketing Department for several years. She still enjoys creative writing but is currently disabled and often in too much pain or exhaustion to write. Thanks, dear heart, for all the love you give me, for I know too often you struggle to smile through your tears.

Acknowledgments

When I was looking for an editor for my first novel, our former pastor came to the rescue. "You don't have to look far," he said, "as I know someone here in the Twin Cities whom I'm sure you'd like." Thank you, *Pastor Don Johnson*. I will be forever grateful to you for helping me find this talented lady whose name is *Mary Lou Sather*.

Thank you, Mary Lou, for agreeing to be my content editor, and for your painstaking critique of this manuscript throughout its crafting. Your eagle eye for detail kept the story from egregious inaccuracies and inconsistencies.

In 1998, I enrolled with the Writer's Digest School and was assigned *Marilyn Meredith* as my instructor. Marilyn is an author who makes her residency in California, and her personality shines through the pages of her numerous novels. It was no easy task to prepare this hopeful for her entrance into the literary world. I was delighted when Marilyn told me I was making swift progress.

I'd be bereft if I didn't acknowledge the patience of many *friends and family* who continually put up with my lack of time to enter into activities they knew I'd enjoy.

BEFORE THE STOCK MARKET
CRASH OF 1929

THE FAMILY ENJOYING A DAY
ON THE BEACH OF LAKE SUPERIOR

JONATHAN and JENNY holding HOLLY
(BELOW) DAVID and MAGGIE

Chapter 1

The Bank Examiners

Laurel Hill, Michigan
1930

Jenny

After the stock market crash in October 1929, with all the horror stories that ensued, I was aware that my husband, Jonathan, spent many evenings working later than usual at the bank. He explained his absences by saying that reviewing the bookkeeping was far more difficult than it had ever been before the crash.

But I was not at all prepared for the shock that came a year later. The morning of that disastrous day that changed all our lives, Jonathan told me the bank examiners were due and he might be late; instead he arrived two hours early. When he slammed the front door, I knew he was more than overcome with fury because his face was beet red. My stomach did cartwheels; something was terribly wrong. Overcome with fear, I asked him, "I thought you were going to be late this evening? What happened?"

"Start packing," he ordered. "We're moving to Duluth as soon as I get a van scheduled."

"Moving?" In shock I cried, "But why?" I couldn't have heard him right because why should we move when our lives were so full here in Laurel Hill?

"I lost my job at the bank," he barked as he pounded up the stairs.

I followed him and stumbled on one step. Why would he lose his job when he had advanced in his career to vice president and a position on the board? What had he done to cause this?

"Lost your job? But why?"

He stopped on the last step and whirled to face me. "Don't ever ask me that again," he thundered, "because I don't intend to discuss this further with you or anyone else."

He charged into our bedroom and slammed the door in my face. I was twelve years younger than this man, always a little in awe of him, frightened of his temper, and ready to do his will; but such fear was nothing compared to what I felt now. He was robbing me of my friends and a most comfortable life and introducing me to the alarming unknown. We had the responsibility of caring for three children, and I was paralyzed with fear at the prospect of doing it with only the money in our pockets.

Start packing? Is that what he said? I don't have the energy to pack a feather.

(One Year Later)

Duluth, Minnesota
1931

Jenny

"Oh, dear God, am I doing the right thing?" I rush down the aisle of the train as if trying to escape someone attempting to do me harm. There are few passengers for which I am grateful because I know that if anyone were to question me as to why I'm so upset, I would surely be unable to retain my composure as tears are already welling up in my eyes.

I stop at a seat not far from the back of the coach and toss my overnight case, purse, and small paper bag in the center seat hoping I will not have to remove them for another traveler.

I wiggle over the seat to be near the window to search for my eight-year-old daughter Maggie and my mother. There they are on the platform, waving. Somehow I manage to return their farewells. They look so sad—two small figures overcome with the grief I've given them. How I ache to hold my precious Maggie in my arms.

Love? How does one define *love*? I love my children, and they return that love unconditionally as I long with all my heart to keep from disappointing them. But my husband? He measures out love in only the portion he decides I should have, and his way of handing out affection leaves me with no desire to return it. There are so many kinds of love and ways to express endearment.

This afternoon, I knew without a doubt what heartbreak was. I hurt Maggie when I knew I must risk her pain for the good of us all, and I certainly didn't expect her to understand. When I had announced that in a few hours I was leaving for Milwaukee, I knew the torment I was giving her, and the whole episode ripped at my conscience. Her cries were like screeching car tires when the driver attempts to prevent an accident, and this pain still rings in my ears.

"Why did you wait to tell me until right before you're leaving, Mama? You've never left me before."

But I knew I couldn't spend days listening to her pleas. When we talked this afternoon, she continued to beg until she realized this was futile and then pleaded, "If you can't stay, Mama, please take me with you."

To her that made sense, but I couldn't put the burden on Ruth. After our conversation, I was emotionally drained and wondered if I would have been able to break away had this discussion continued much longer. It's always heartbreaking for me to see anyone suffer, but how much more agonizing it is to witness my tormented daughter hurting like this.

Another day in Duluth would have been unbearable, so I had no choice but to leave. The same questions were hurled continuously at me from friends and family, and it was difficult to hold back my feelings. “Where is your husband?” “Why did you leave Laurel Hill when we all thought you were happy there?” “Will you and your family make your home in Duluth when Jonathan gets back?” I had no desire to tell my tragic tale to anyone.

When Ruth’s letter came from Milwaukee a little over a week ago, I was genuinely surprised. I had not seen nor heard from my cousin in years. I stared at the invitation that asked me to visit until I suddenly became aware Ruth had not stated when I should come or how long I was welcome. It was then I realized this could be my opportunity to leave Duluth and look for work in Milwaukee, a much larger city where there would surely be a greater chance for finding a job. My success in locating employment in Duluth with the scarcity of jobs during this Great Depression had been futile despite my experience in the retail field. I feared I wouldn’t have enough money to pay our monthly life insurance fees should anything happen to Jonathan or me, and then what would happen to our children?

Leaving Duluth was not without problems. Who would care for David, Holly, and Maggie? The very thought of solving this dilemma drove a deep chill within me since I would have to find three homes so that the the burden would not fall on any one household. It would be difficult for any family to sacrifice what little they have to care for even one child in these bad times.

Could this be one answer? Jonathan’s sister Alma and her husband, Jake, might possibly be right for David. With no children of their own, they could be thrilled to care for our handsome six-year-old son David. When I asked them, they agreed so rapidly that I was actually startled. Instead of being comforted, it was as if they were grabbing my son from my arms, and I wondered if I had made the right choice.

Perhaps three-year-old Holly would be worth the sacrifice of some of their resources, but only if it wouldn’t be too much trouble for my mother-in-law and her son Elmer. Would they care for her? I knew Grandma Westin saw her daughter Alma often, and the blessing of this arrangement would be that the siblings would benefit from frequent visits and spend welcome time together. It was truly a relief when they did not falter, and both mother and son agreed without hesitation. I knew they loved Holly who is such a calm and good youngster that she would brighten their days as she had always lifted our spirits. I had no doubt they would be kind to her.

But Maggie? She's the oldest and is far more sensitive than the other two children. I can think of no alternative for my eight-year-old daughter than to leave her with my sister Marie and her husband, Carl, but even that decision has a stumbling block. Adjusting to Marie and her rules will be extremely difficult for Maggie. Deep down I believe Marie loves the child especially since she was the firstborn in this generation of our family, and Marie doted on Maggie at least until her son Tommy was born. Now I wonder if she is capable of loving anyone but him.

She accuses me of spoiling Maggie. I've watched Marie with her son who obeys his mother because he knows he must, but I have always taught Maggie to do things for me because she loves me and respects my judgment. Thank heavens Marie and her family live in Mother's home where our mother needs their support for company and their help to pay the mortgage. In turn, Marie and her family need a place to live. I pray that Mother will be Maggie's shelter when circumstances get rough and this vulnerable child faces all the changes in her life.

I make the necessary arrangements for our children and then decide it might be best to wait until I get to Milwaukee to ask my cousin Ruth if she and her husband will allow me to stay with them until I find work. When I'm successful, I can rent a room of my own, so I pack my personal belongings and ship them to Ruth a week ahead of my arrival without notifying her. The huge box must be there by now, and the remaining time before I leave is limited. I'm concerned that Ruth and her husband will be puzzled and wonder if the large size of the box indicates how long I will be staying with them.

Not until the day before I board the train do I send a telegram informing Ruth of the time of my arrival. I haven't seen her in years, and it's possible she's changed and might find a reason to say no to my coming at this time. There is a greater possibility that her husband will not agree to the arrangement.

What if I can't find a job in a short while? I do not even have the money to return to Duluth, and the thought of that terrifies me and ruffles my pride. I must leave Duluth soon, or I might lose my nerve and back out of this escape to Milwaukee where I'm thankful there are no kinfolk and friends with their prying and endless questions.

The clatter of the train's wheels vibrates on the tracks, and the noise pounds in my ears. I catch my last glimpse of Mother and Maggie, and an emptiness fills me as the train picks up speed, and we move through the West End where I grew up. What happy days when my cousin Ruth and I were inseparable and filled our days sharing our dreams. What joy we knew as children when we did not have a care in the world.

The train crosses over into Wisconsin, and as it winds around a curve, I catch a fleeting glimpse of a small portion of Duluth in the remote distance. Elevation is higher in the eastern end of the city that overlooks Lake Superior, and many splendid homes that only the rich can afford were built in that area before the 1929 crash. Darkness is drifting in now, along with what seems to be a developing fog that happens often in Duluth. The streetlights flicker through the mist as if flirting with me.

I grasp the paper sack Mother handed me when I boarded the train, and I'm sure it's something to eat. She was upset at supper tonight when I picked at my food because she believes the cure for all ailments, physical and mental, is nourishment. I stare at the meatball sandwich on her homemade bread and know that even though Mother is an excellent cook, my mouth feels like straw and the smell of food makes me ill. I drop the sandwich back into the bag and crumple the top in order to return it to the empty seat beside me. Maybe if I shut my eyes, the motion of the railway car will help me relax.

Confused and forgetting where I am, I feel my body jump. Did I doze off?

"Tickets, please," a high-pitched voice echoes through the railway car, and again in a more forceful, almost singing voice I hear a repeated "Tickets."

The pudgy uniformed man is waddling down the aisle accepting something from each outstretched hand, and I'm finally awake enough to realize he is punching tickets. Where did I put my fare? As he draws nearer, I panic and wildly fumble through my purse in a frantic search for the voucher. With a sigh of relief, I hand him the ticket that will take me to Milwaukee and my dear cousin Ruth.

My disturbed mind will not let me doze off again, and disastrous events swirl before my eyes. I feel I have no power over them when they hold me captive while I view my agonizing past as if it were on a silent movie screen. But when my past and present collide, I review my recent venomous memories again, so perhaps it will give me some relief if I recall a happier time.

Were there cheerful periods during our marriage? Oh yes. A few years after we were married, Jonathan received the letter that changed the course of our lives, and I observed he wore a true sense of relief as he read it. Four months before this, he had lost his job as a bookkeeper at the Duluth Furniture Store in West End, and we could no longer pay the rent or buy groceries. Finding another job in Duluth was exceedingly difficult. We knew if this lack of employment continued we would have to beg both our parents to take us in, hoping at least one family would open their arms and accept us. It was then that Jon's cousin George, who holds the position of vice president in the largest bank in downtown Duluth, learned of an opening in Laurel Hill, Michigan, where Jonathan did not hesitate to heed his advice to travel for an interview.

When he returned, Jon was exceedingly excited and described the surrounding area before telling me the bank was located in a small but charming town near the shores of Lake Superior in Upper Michigan. He said it seemed like a dream, but he was nevertheless hopeful that he would get the assignment. His colorful description of the community and its location was so enticing that I was not only praying Jon would get work but was caught up in the excitement of our probable adventure.

The letter he held in his hand read that he was being offered the position of teller, and I was so thrilled that I jumped up from my chair and threw my arms around him. Our move meant being away from my family, but even though I would have to give up their companionship for now, I'd welcome their visits. I was thrilled the day the good news came and I packed with intense speed and said goodbye to loved ones in Duluth. Daughter Maggie was two years old at the time—a tiny child, bright for her years. It would be a new beginning for us and that it unquestionably was for some time before everything slid downhill with the speed of a sled on an icy hill.

What did the 1929 stock market crash do to our lives?

More realistically, what did my husband, Jon, do to our family? My mind silently screams that I hate him, but perhaps it's not really hate; however, believing it now helps to consume some of my anger. Emotionally drained, I lean my head against the red velvet seat of the railway car.

Although he has never told me what happened, I feel in my heart that Jonathan must have committed some crime, whatever that might be, and my fear is that folks in Duluth would believe I drove him to do it. It isn't true, but people do enjoy gossip and point "guilty" fingers at the innocent.

Oh, Jonathan, you are such a charmer that no one would ever believe you would do anything wrong.

Not aware I had dozed off, I open my eyes and look outside. It's now dark, and I feel tired though I must have slept some. A man occupying one of the seats in front of me is snoring with intensity that's great enough to keep the whole car awake. Thank heavens I'm not married to him. But what am I thinking? Living with someone who snores is nothing compared to my nightmare. Does anyone besides me know of Jon's unpredictable temper? It is no wonder I am so afraid of him. A couple years ago, he read an item in the gossip column of the local newspaper that only hinted he was having an affair. When he read it, he jumped up, ripped the paper, and hurled it into the fireplace as if he were a baseball pitcher. His lack of control disturbed me, but I believe there was little threat in what the article states about Jonathan as he is a family man. He would never stray from his dynasty to have an affair. Never.

Jonathan joined several of the most important businessmen in town to develop plans to open a golf course. When it was completed and opened, I played at the new club regularly with the wives of the postmaster, chief of police, and many of my bridge club friends. No one was more amazed than I when one afternoon I made a hole in one. When Jonathan learned this, he lost his temper and ruined a new golf club by swinging and cracking it into a tree with the strength of his anger. I was puzzled and wondered if it was his chauvinistic mind-set that believed how dare a woman outplay him at a "man's game," or was it but his uncontrollable temper?

Chapter 2

Left Behind

Maggie

I stand on the train platform, staring at the window where I see Mama. She's still waving to us, but my arm is so tired that I can't do this anymore, so I throw her a kiss. The huge locomotive begins to move, and I let out a cry because I know I can't stop the train. It lurches and chugs down the track, and my hand falls limply to my side as it rolls out of sight taking away my precious mama whom I love most in all the world. A large sob is about to leap from my mouth, but I try my best to keep it in so I won't upset Grandma Nelly who holds my hand and guides me up the hill to the trolley stop.

A cold wind whirls around us as we wait on the corner, and I shake for what seems forever until a rumbling streetcar comes toward us and stops so we can climb the high steps to enter. Grandma puts in tokens that clink when she drops them in the box before she turns to lead me behind the conductor to two long benches that face each other. No one is sitting across from us, and I'm glad because I can feel the tears beginning to tickle my cheeks, and I don't want anyone to think I'm a baby. The streetcar rumbles as it takes us out of downtown on its way to the place where I must now live without my family.

As I sit watching but not really seeing the buildings and houses we pass, I remember how happy we were in our big house in Laurel Hill until that terrible day when Daddy said we had to move to Duluth. When I asked why, he got so mad he made me quiver but later told me it had something to do with the stock market crash—whatever that is. How can something crashing mean everything has to change? Will our family ever be together again? It makes me so darned scared it won't happen that I shake my head to get the thought out. All the way out.

When we reach our stop, Grandma gets off first and helps me down. She's very quiet as we drag our feet for three blocks up the rising hill to her house. The wind off the lake blows so hard that it whistles in my ears, and then I hear a rumbling sound like thunder in the distance.

"Can I go right to bed, Grandma? I just don't feel like talking to anyone."

"Yes, dear, of course, and I will join you after I stop to talk to Auntie Marie and Uncle Carl." But what she says next makes me very upset. "You will have to sleep with me in my bed, though."

"Can't I sleep where Mama and I slept before she left?"

"No, Maggie, because your aunt Marie wants to use that for a guest room and told me she'd move your clothes in with mine tomorrow."

When we get to Grandma's house, I go right up the stairs and into her room. My pajamas are already on the bed, and I suppose Auntie Marie couldn't wait to put them there. After I take off my clothes, I fold them neatly like Mama taught me; then I carefully put them on the rocking chair before I slowly crawl under the rough sheets. I hug my pillow pretending it is Mama and try to sleep, but all I can think about is what happened when she told me she was going away. That keeps going over and over in my head and won't get out.

We were in the back yard, and I still hear Mama saying to me, "Maggie, sit by me so we can discuss this." I hear her patting the porch step as I stand motionless on the wooden sidewalk. I don't want to talk so I turn and squint at Uncle Carl's pink, purple, and red sweet peas. Their thin, green feelers cling to a trellis the way I struggle to keep Mama with me. I move closer to finger the fragrant butterfly-shaped flowers, but I know I'm only trying to avoid Mama's eyes and her touch. This has never happened before, but something strange is churning inside me. Before today I never doubted her love, but now I wonder if she really does care about me. I love her with all my heart, but does she love *me* that much? None of this makes sense because if she must go away, why doesn't she take me with her? I don't understand nothin'.

"Maggie, please," Mama pleads as I stay where I am because she broke my heart when she announced she was leaving—just like Daddy left us before I knew what was happening. Then one day my sister and brother were gone, but at least Mama was still here. Without her, am I going to crumple?

I choke back tears and am angry now in a new, strong way. Mama told me Daddy's sister Alma gets that way when her husband is on his way home from work but turns before he gets there and goes to a place called a tavern. When he finally gets home, she throws things at him. I could never throw anything at Mama no matter how mad I got at her.

Finally, I spin around to face her. "Why are you leaving me? How can you be so mean?" Then I stop because now for the first time I'm saying things without thinking about the words first. Maybe I can't help it when I get so frightened.

Mama holds out her arms to me. She seems sad, the saddest I have ever seen her, but I'm too troubled to be comforted even if I miss the warmth of her arms. Why is this happening? Overcome, I stumble toward her and fall into her arms and sob.

"Oh, Maggie, Maggie," she says as she rocks me gently. After several minutes, I rest my cheek on her shoulder not caring if my tears make her pretty dress wet. My insides feel like they have rocks in there, and I find little comfort from her. I know for sure that I've never felt like this before.

She gently wipes her soft white handkerchief with the lace corners over my damp cheek as I gaze into her eyes. They usually twinkle with fun and mischief, always seeking something to laugh about, but today there are no smiles or laughter—only endless sadness that I have never seen there before.

"How can you leave me alone?" I ask again.

Mama wrinkles her brow and says, "But, Maggie, you won't be alone. Your Grandma Nelly, Uncle Carl, and Aunt Marie are here to care for you." Surprised by her words, I stare at her. Does she really think living with them is like living with her? They aren't my family; they're only relatives.

Maybe Mama is having that problem of going through some kind of change like when her lady friends don't know I'm near, and I hear them talking about people like that. They say women go mad and need to go to a sanitary place. Before today Mama always said the smartest things, but now nothing makes sense. If it's true she's going mad, I want to go with her even to that awful place where they send ladies.

I draw away from her and stomp down the sidewalk to kick a stone. It swirls into the air and I watch it fall into Uncle Carl's neatly cut grass. Everything about this house and yard is like a rich lady's living room that you can peek into but are not allowed to enter.

I have to help her understand. "When other people take care of me, Mama, it isn't the same. Doggone it—what's this all about? You won't explain what's wrong," I shout as I stamp my foot. "It must be a big secret because things keep changing. First, Daddy goes away . . . hey, where is he anyway? You've never told me where Daddy went." She hesitates as if about to answer, but I'm too nervous to wait. Instead, I ask, "Why is everything changing?"

"Really, Maggie, you're only eight years old, and I don't expect you to understand."

Who does Mama think I am, some little kid? I always understand when she explains things to me, so why can't she tell me this?

"These are hard times, honey. We're going through the Great Depression and have been caught in the middle. That means everyone has very little money to live on." Mama is speaking so softly I can barely hear her. "After Daddy lost his job, he had many problems and had to go to Illinois. He had no choice." She stops and then speaks slowly as she nods her head and says again, "He just had too many problems." Mama turns her face away, and for the first time, I realize she is sad too; maybe almost as scared as I am.

"Mama, once I think you told me he'd gone to someplace like Illinois. Where is Illinois anyway?" I'd better find that jigsaw puzzle of the United States and fit all the states together so I can find it. I'm thinking so hard about so much that my head feels like it will burst wide open, and what an icky mess that would make.

"Sometime when you're older, dear, we'll talk about this. For now, know that Milwaukee is between Duluth and Illinois. When I can save the money, I'll visit both you and Daddy."

I guess I haven't thought much about Mama's feelings. Is it possible that she really doesn't want to leave us? But she isn't helping me feel better by telling me I'm a little kid, and she needs to know I do understand. I move closer so I can reach out and touch her because now I'm seeing her kinda different as if maybe she hurts bad like me.

A cold wind comes out of nowhere, and I shiver. Uncle Carl, who knows about things like this, said that in Duluth the temperature can go down quickly without warning like twenty degrees in less than fifteen minutes. He probably has it all measured out somewhere. First, the air is hot like Grandma's stove, and then a wind he calls a northerly races like a speedboat across Lake Superior. When it reaches the shore, the whole city shivers as the cold swoops down like a giant hungry bird that's diving after a worm, and you suddenly need a sweater. That's how my insides feel right now; everything changing as fast as the northerly air.

"Mama, why can't my brother and sister live here with me? David and Holly would give me some family while you and Daddy are away."

My mother draws me to her again, offering protection from the wind. "Carl and Marie can't afford to take care of all three of you," she explains, "and it breaks my heart to separate you children. But it costs money to raise you, and I'm fortunate our relatives will help so I don't have to temporarily put you in an orphanage. Anyway, you'll have Tommy to play with."

"Mama," I shout, truly defeated as I jump up to face her. "Tommy is four years old, and he's only a cousin. And why did you wait until this afternoon to tell me? Did you just now decide to go?"

She shakes her head. "No, dear. A couple weeks ago my cousin Ruth in Milwaukee invited me to visit her. I can find work in that big city so much easier than here. But I had to find a place for your brother and sister first. You remember Auntie Alma, Daddy's sister, and her husband Jake? They agreed to take David, and I truly believe they were happy about that as they have no children of their own. Thankfully Grandma Westin will care for Holly. Don't you see, dear, it's the only way I can save money for us to be together?"

Now this is the first time Mama has made sense, but making sense doesn't always make people feel better.

She goes inside now, and I promise to come in soon. I wonder how long she will be in Milwaukee and who will have charge of me? Grandma is nice, but she is old. Uncle Carl? No, he hardly knows me. Then suddenly it becomes clear, and I draw in a big breath. Oh no, not Auntie Marie. "Mama, Auntie is so strict." I cry now in pain, "Please, please don't go."

But she won't listen to me.

The painful scene fades, and big tears I have been trying to hold back start to flow. I want to sleep, but I'm too restless until I feel a thump at the bottom of the bed and know it's the little stray cat who begged at our door last week. His sad big eyes made me want to pet the precious guy and open the latch, but my feelings did not count with Auntie Marie. When her Tommy wiggled his way near me and cried to his mother to let the cat in, she finally said, "All right, but only until someone claims him."

It's too dark to see Ted Bear now, but I have memorized how he looks. He's a small cat with lots of rust and white fur, a pointed nose, big ears, and the cutest white fur collar under his chin. I named him Ted Bear because he reminds me of a teddy bear. Now his warm body snuggles up to me as if he wants to tell me, "Don't be sad. I'm here."

I pet him and feel his little body grow limp. I sense my tears are still coming because he does the strangest thing. His tiny paw reaches for my face, and he brushes a tear from my cheek. I'm so surprised that I hug his little body to me.

"Oh, Ted Bear, you do know how much I hurt."

When I have to go potty, I tuck the blanket over Ted Bear and tiptoe down the hall to the bathroom. When I'm finished, I don't even pull the long steel string to flush because someone might hear it and know I'm still awake. Voices seem to be coming from somewhere, and when I glance down at the slotted grate on the floor next to the toilet, I believe it's coming from there. Can I move the latch to open it a little? I get down on my hands and knees and move it very slowly, without any noise, and see a little of the kitchen below me. Yes, there's Auntie Marie, Uncle Carl, and Grandma Nelly sitting around the kitchen table.

"I suppose you want to know if Jenny caught the train on time," I hear Grandma says. "Yah, she did."

Uncle Carl looks at her. "How I wish we'd been able to buy that secondhand automobile, Mother. I hated to send you and Maggie downtown on the streetcar and then have you catch another to get home."

He makes me smile 'cause he's so nice. I hope Uncle Carl gets a car soon because it certainly would have helped us tonight. Now Auntie Marie says something, so I put my ear closer to listen.

"Mother, we want you to know about the discussion Carl and I had tonight regarding money. You and I know that men don't like their wives working because it embarrasses them since they believe a woman's place is in the home. As you know, Carl has been most understanding about my working part-time, but now with another mouth to feed, it might be wise if I seek a full-time bookkeeping job. Jenny says she'll send money, but how can she when she'd have to send to all three families who care for her children plus supporting herself?

"Here's what I need you to understand, Mother. My working full-time can only happen if you're willing to care for the children while I'm at work. That will put additional responsibility on you, so be sure to tell me how you honestly feel. Are you willing to do this?"

Grandma Nelly answers right away, "You know how much I love both Tommy and Maggie, and I'll take pleasure in caring for them. Yes, that will be just fine."

This is the best thing I've heard today—Auntie Marie won't be here during the day. Then I realize I'd better get back to the bedroom before Grandma comes upstairs.

A few minutes later she enters the room, and I pretend I'm asleep. I've stopped crying, but I don't want to talk to anyone. I'll betcha Grandma knows that the cat is in the bed where he's not allowed, but she says nothing. Instead, I hear her make a big sigh as she pulls the covers over herself and turns away from Ted Bear and me. I know she's crying because I can feel the bed shake, which makes me want to reach out to comfort her, but I honest-to-goodness don't know how. Grandma is so nice but keeps her hugs and feelings way down deep inside, and how I wish she wouldn't do that.

When I think Grandma Nelly is asleep, I pet Ted Bear and listen to his soft purring. When he jumps down and goes away, I turn on my side. Again, the tears flow until finally the sandman comes.

Chapter 3

Arrival in Milwaukee

Jenny

The swaying and jerking of the railway car awakens me, and I become aware of the pain in my neck, shoulders, and back from sitting in such an uncomfortable position. As I stretch my body, my eyes catch the first rays of sun to break through the streaks of gossamer clouds that adorn the early-morning sky. Too soon the pain of the preceding day penetrates my thoughts, and I quickly close my eyes, but it erases nothing from my memory for it's all too real.

My first concern is for Maggie and if she will be able to adjust to my sister Marie whose personality changes when she has responsibility. Then she's the one in control and woe be unto anyone who attempts to shake her from her throne.

How perfectly she fits the role of a career woman even to the tailored dresses and stiff white collars she wears to the office. I've witnessed her efficiency at home where she is a meticulous housekeeper and surely must be the same neat person at the office. I cannot say the same for myself maybe because I had so many years of help from the two teenage sisters who worked for us in Michigan.

The girls lived on a farm and were most anxious to attend school in our town. Since we had a spare bedroom off the kitchen, we furnished them with free room and board plus spending money while they, in turn, did many tasks around our home. I treasured both girls, and the work arrangement gave me time to support my husband socially by befriending the prominent women in our community. I have always enjoyed people, so this was pure pleasure for me. We took our bridge club to different towns in Upper Michigan to meet with and challenge their groups.

My sister Marie might be strict but is quite different when she is having fun. Then her vivid brown eyes sparkle, and a smile lights up her face as she emerges an amusing woman. Her laugh is so contagious that others enjoy her presence. I fear that having the responsibility of Maggie will not help either Marie or the child, and that concerns me because I'm powerless at this time to do anything to alter that.

Marie loves her three-year-old son, Tommy, but she is too strict with him. She expresses her love by giving him gifts and then forcing his appreciation. That's not giving him the right message, and I pity Tommy because he lacks the physical love of a mother who holds her child in her arms until he or she senses her endearment.

Now the voice comes loud and clear: "Milwaukee. Next stop Milwaukee."

Passengers pull suitcases from the upper baggage racks, and I am presently even more grateful that I sent most of my luggage ahead and am not laboring with heavy bags. Hopefully the large box I mailed last week has arrived by now. I stand to smooth the wrinkles from my brown dress skirt when I'm suddenly thrown forward and must clutch the seat in front of me to steady myself. When the train comes to a complete halt, I pick up my small carry-on case and anxiously follow several people to the front exit.

The conductor walks ahead to descend the steps and slaps a footstool at his feet before bellowing to the travelers in a singsong voice, "Watch your step." He extends his hand to assist them to balance themselves as they leave the coach, and I thank him as my feet meet the wooden platform before turning in search of cousin Ruth.

I study the crowd for some time but do not see her. What if she did not get my telegram? Perhaps she and Cliff were angry when my luggage arrived with no explanation. Without a doubt, their invitation was for a short visit, and all my belongings must have perplexed them. Could it be they have guessed I want to stay longer so I'm not welcome?

Perhaps I cannot see Ruth because there are so many people, but when I perceive a waving arm farther down the platform I truly pray that it's my cousin.

Somehow, she does not look like the Ruth I remember. She's put on weight, and her long, blond tresses have been pulled straight back, giving her a severe look that is not familiar to me. Then she smiles with such warmth that I know that happy look would warm a frozen soul. Ruth reaches out to pull me to her and gives me a hug that reassures me she isn't upset at my sending my clothes ahead without giving an explanation for my action. It could be that she recalls how much I dislike writing letters.

"I'm so thrilled you are finally here, Jenny, and having someone to visit with as dear as you are to me will be heavenly. It's been a long time since we've had a good talk."

Ruth grasps my hand and takes the small suitcase from me. "Your luggage arrived yesterday," she says. I don't know what to say but realize Ruth is probably curious.

"We have only one automobile, Jenny, and Cliff has that. Do you mind if we take the streetcar?

It's a half-hour ride, but the time passes quickly. At our stop, the conductor opens the folding doors, and we cling to the railing as we descend the steps. Tempting smells permeate my senses that must have come from the bakery on the corner, and I realize that I am actually hungry. Ruth explains that their apartment is directly above the pastry shop, and she leads the way up a flight of steps to the next floor. When she opens the door, I see a sizable room and am encouraged to make myself at home while she picks up Becky from her next-door neighbor who has been caring for her during her absence.

Moments later, Ruth reappears and sets Becky down on the kitchen floor where the youngster dashes behind her mother and grabs her floral skirt to hide from this complete stranger. It's indeed apparent that Becky is very shy.

She peeks from behind Ruth's skirt and is gazing at me. Her brown hair is parted in the center and tied back with ribbons to hold spiraling ringlets. Her radiant dark eyes would mesmerize anyone, but when she finally smiles at me, I entertain two reactions. I certainly am happy she is warming up, but at the same time, a wave of longing for my own children washes over me. When I regain my composure, I direct questions to the little one.

"I bet you're three years old, aren't you?"

"No," she snaps. "Me dis many," and she holds up two tiny fingers.

"You're only two? I can tell she's taken back by my unusual reaction. "But, Becky, you're so smart for your age. Do you suppose that since you're that old, you can give me a big hug?" But the child grasps her mother's hand. Not yet, I guess.

"She's almost three," Ruth tells me, "and when she gets up to speed, you'll notice she talks so much that you'll wish she would stop exercising her lungs."

"Should we show Jenny the apartment, Becky?" Ruth smiles at her daughter as she encourages her to agree.

The child studies me once again, then beckons me to follow her on a grand tour that her mother leads. I'm shown every portion of the kitchen with its small pantry, and I stop by the window to gaze at a sizable park. The dining area is shown next where I see an old wooden table and four matching chairs. Becky shyly points to the corner of the room where she has a small table of her own with two tiny chairs and several doll dishes and toys.

The living room is small but cheerful. We only glance from the entrance into Cliff and Ruth's bedroom, but when we approach Becky's room, she points to it to inform me, "Dis yurs," then dashes away to stand near the bathroom to entice me to view the last room.

I turn to Ruth and tell her that I don't want to put the child out of her bedroom, but she's quick to assure me they've borrowed a small bed to put in their room and Becky is excited about sleeping there.

"I explained to her how crowded everything was when we were children," Ruth says.

"That's putting it mildly." A joyous feeling of closeness sweeps over me with the memory.

"Yes, and we didn't mind, did we?"

After Ruth leads Becky back to her play area, we return to the kitchen where my cousin puts on a pot of water to prepare tea. She buzzes around getting cups and delicious-looking bakery rolls while my mind enters the memory door she just opened.

As children, Ruth and I were not only cousins but the best of friends when our families lived in the same residence in Duluth's West End in a large three-story house shared by three immigrant families. Ruth's family occupied the top floor, Dad's relatives were on the second floor, and my family lived on the main floor with its two bedrooms, a dining area, a kitchen, and a living room. An enclosed porch completed our lodging, but it was necessary to close it off during the cold winter months to keep out drafts. When Christmas celebrations were over, the decorated tree was moved to that porch where the cold air kept it fragrant and green until spring. It was then that the trimmings were packed, and the tree was hauled away.

Our kitchen on this main floor was of necessity shared by all the residents. Each family accepted a different hour to prepare and eat their meal with the exception being a special occasion when all three families participated by bringing food to share and then gathering to enjoy the delicious meal and friendly conversation.

"Do you remember all the crazy things we used to do?" Ruth asks as she leads me from memory lane to the present.

"How could I ever forget? Those were some of the most fun days of my life."

We talk for hours over many cups of tea and matching interruptions from Becky. I ask my cousin how she knew where to contact me. Ruth said she was sure my mother would forward the letter if she sent it to her, but there was no need since I was already residing there.

Ruth inquires about my children, her other relatives, and even Jonathan though there is little I want to share with her about him at this time. I inform Ruth that I would like to stay in Milwaukee for now to look for work.

"Would you mind if I live here until I find a job and save sufficient money to rent a room?"

Ruth grins. "When your clothes arrived, I guessed you had that in mind. I talked to Cliff who said that if that's your plan, he has no problem with it.

"I saved the newspaper for you," Ruth says as she hands it to me. "There's an ad for a saleswoman at one of our downtown department stores. Are you interested?" She knows that before I married Jon, I worked in the women's department at the well-known Glass Block Department Store in the heart of Duluth's downtown district.

"There's only one problem," Ruth continues. "Cliff has signed up to take the balance of his vacation in a couple weeks so we can spend the time at a resort. We've invited my mother and little sister Dolores to join us. They live close to Onalaska now."

"Don't worry about me," I tell her. "Tomorrow I'll apply for the job and see if they'll hire me."

When the supervisor learns of the experience I've had, I have no difficulty getting hired by Schuster's. But as time progresses, I'm not sure how long I can stand the agony of the job. The days continue to be hot and sticky, and the heat intensifies inside the building because the numerous ceiling fans are unable to adequately cool the huge areas in the store. My legs ache and my feet are miserable and throb constantly. Too frequently our dressing rooms are occupied by perspiring women whose often unwashed bodies send off an unbearable stench of body odor. Each day drags on endlessly until the store closes, and the staff is set free from our agony.

Employees who join me at the car stop express relief to get out into the late-afternoon air because at times a slight breeze comes off the cool waters of Lake Michigan. Even if that doesn't happen, at least the air is fresher outdoors than inside the building.

One sweltering Friday evening, I pick up an order of food at Schuster's famous German delicatessen. As I leave the building, I am fortunate the streetcar I must take is rumbling toward me. I am breathless after climbing the familiar stairs to Ruth and Cliff's apartment and discover when I open the door that all windows are open with fans circulating the unrelenting heat through the living room and kitchen. Even Becky has little of her usual energy.

"I'm so thankful for this food," Ruth tells me as she takes the package from me. "This morning when you said you'd supply the meal tonight, I didn't realize at that early hour how grateful I'd be by evening. The heat has completely taken over this building, and I certainly don't feel like cooking tonight. Cliff is German and will be pleased with your choice of potato salad and wurst."

I change into a housedress and help Ruth set the table. From time to time, we take turns standing in front of a fan.

"So how was work today?"

"Oh, Ruth, I've got to look for something else," I say as I flop into a chair. "I thought I could take this but until the department stores put in this new system called air-conditioning, it's too much. I've never done anything but sell clothing, but there must be something else I can do."

It is quiet for a few moments until Ruth suggests, "Well, you've raised children, haven't you?"

"Of course, but you know that. And what has children got to do with my finding a job?"

"Look through the want ads," Ruth continues. "Many shrewd businessmen made good financial choices before the stock market crash and were not caught up in the horror of this Great Depression. They now remain in their luxurious castles and need many employees to keep the homes running smoothly and provide care for their families. Jenny, you'd make a great employee with your love of youngsters and the way they take to you. With any luck, you might even find something by the time we get back from our vacation, but right now, I can hardly wait for Sunday so we can leave for that resort and cool off." Ruth sits in the chair next to me and wipes her forehead.

I turn the pages of the newspaper she has given me to the want ad section before promising myself that I'll find another job as soon as possible. Why not give my notice to Schusters on Monday? Anything should be better than working in that sweltering building.

Chapter 4

It's Different Here Now

Maggie

I wander into the kitchen and drop into one of Grandma's wooden chairs before sensing a drop of perspiration trickling down my nose. I run the back of my hand over it.

"Maggie, don't you have a handkerchief?" Auntie Marie asks. I know she's angry because her voice is so mean.

"Guess I left it in the pocket of my other dress."

"Then you'd better remember to transfer it to the outfit you're wearing now," she says in "that" voice that would scare a tiger.

Auntie Marie doesn't stop long enough for me to answer her before she gives her first order. I know she does not care what I think or want, so she dishes out instructions like they plop mashed potatoes on the plates of hungry people in the soup-and-food lines. *Plop, plop, plop.* I've seen pictures of those men in the newspaper. They need food and someplace to sleep while trying to find a job.

"Better change your clothes." *Plop* go the potatoes.

"Today you're excused from kitchen duties because I want you to watch Tommy while Grandma and I get dinner." *Plop.*

"Go." She barely takes a breath before the next order comes. "Be sure to hang up your dress." *Plop.*

"Maggie, did you wear your good shoes today? Do you think we're made of money? What were you thinking?"

I hang my head.

"Change your shoes." *Plop*.

"I've moved the rest of your clothes from the guest room you shared with your mother to the back bedroom where you're going to sleep with Grandma from now on. Now go upstairs and hang them up. Get busy." *Plop*.

I can tell she intends I have no time for myself, so I walk slowly down the narrow reception hall. I like this grand room near the front door where people sit to be comfortable while they wait for the person they came to visit. I study the two chairs in here and the long, high library table with books on each end. The two lamps on top of the table are gorgeous, and Mama told me the shades are stained glass.

What Auntie calls a coat tree stands by the front door, and it has a rubber mat under it for rubbers in the summer and overshoes in the winter. I turn the corner to climb the stairs, pulling myself up by grabbing the railing. When I reach the top, I begin my stroll to the end of the hall.

When I near the door of the pretty room that I slept in with Mama, I stop and stare. Why won't Auntie let Grandma and me sleep in this room? I thought this was Grandma's house, but maybe I'm wrong and it belongs to Auntie Marie and Uncle Carl. Auntie calls it the guest room which is funny because when Daddy left and Mama and I slept here for a few months, no guests came—unless we were guests? Now guess I'm not even that.

Grandma's room, which I've nicknamed "the dungeon" because it is dark and gloomy with only one window facing the back yard, is to the right. I stare at the tall, old wooden dresser near me and notice the uncomfortable rocking chair beside it as if it is daring me to sit in it and ride. But I moan as I look at the ancient dull brass bed that might not be so bad if it didn't have sagging springs and a lumpy mattress. I always hated that bed, and now I have to sleep in it every night. One thing is for sure. When I get to be a grown-up, I will never, never buy or sleep in a brass bed. So there.

I change my clothes and hang them in the closet as Auntie ordered before putting on my canvas slippers. They are so ugly, but Mama said they will save on my shiny Mary Jane shoes that she insisted I must keep nice as long as they fit. Guess I had better not complain.

I run my fingers through my straight, chestnut hair and wish there was a mirror in this room. I hate straight hair. To make matters worse, mine is short with dumb old straight bangs across my forehead. Why don't I have naturally curly hair? Mama used to fix my hair in rags or curl it with the curling iron she heated on the wood stove. Grandma probably doesn't even know how to do that, and Auntie Marie certainly would not take time to help me because as far as she's concerned my hair is just right the way it is. Uncle Carl calls it a soldier's haircut because it is so neat. Remembering this, I mess it up good with both hands.

They call short girls in my class shrimps, and I am probably the shortest one there. Like lightning, Mama's words flash into my mind. "The best things in life come in small packages," she used to say. Like magic, I remember her words and feel warm and cozy inside. Mama always fixes my sad thinking in no time, but then I remember I am only hearing a memory, and it shrinks me back to my real size.

After I finish dressing, I feel like being naughty and sneak into Auntie Marie's room even though she told me not to go in there. I walk over to the dressing table in the corner of this giant room and then hear a loud voice come from downstairs.

"For goodness sakes, Margaret. What is taking you so long? I told you I want you to play with Tommy."

I know that was Auntie Marie, and I shudder. Why can't she call me Maggie? I know when she uses my whole name that I am in trouble. As quiet as I can, I dash to the stair railing and yell, "I'll be down in a minute, Auntie. I just have to go to the bathroom." Instead, I go back to her bedroom and join the big doll resting on her bed to play with her ruffled pink dress before I run my finger through her curly hair and stroke her fluffy bonnet.

"How I wish Auntie Marie would let me play with you," I whisper. That would be so much fun. Do you remember when I was only five years old, and we had our picture taken together? Now you sit here having no fun just like me because your mother is afraid I will get you dirty. She should know I would take good care of you. It seems nothing in this house is for making people happy.

I know I must go downstairs even though I cannot stand playing with that little Tommy. But as I start down, I hear my cousin giggle. Why is he doing that? Then I see him with his girlish curls tossing in all directions while he plays with Ted Bear. It is not what I expected, and I cannot wait to join him. What surprises me most is that I even feel good about the job Auntie has given me. However, I quickly change my mind when I see Tommy pull the cat's tail.

"Don't you dare hurt him, Tommy," I scream like I am the boss of this house and he had better mind me. Startled, Tommy stares at me and then runs into the dining room to follow the squealing cat.

"What's going on out there?" Auntie Marie yells from the kitchen.

"Oh, nothing—at least nothing much," I tell her. "It's just that Tommy didn't mean to step on the cat's tail but he did. Don't worry, though, because everything is okay now." This is the second teeny-weeny lie I've told, but I'm finding I just have to turn the truth around sometimes. I do not mean to hurt anyone, but I have to take care of myself.

I coax the cat back into the living room with the help of the lace from my canvas shoe, and then Ted Bear goes wild. He spins round and round as he chases the shoelace. Then he goes after his long, slinky tail that leaps away when he jumps to attack it. Before long, he forgets the shoelace and spins in a circle like he is going nuts. I giggle as I watch him try to capture his own built-in cat toy. I do not think he even knows it is attached to him and always out of reach.

Ted Bear snatches the tip of his tail and bites hard. That unexpected pain really scares him, and he leaps into the air. His fur plumps to make him look twice as big as he is. Tommy and I howl like old friends sharing the same joke, and our stomachs hurt from the joy of too much laughter. But then Ted Bear's puffed fur tells me he's going crazy again.

Without stopping, the cat goes wild. He grabs his tail and licks it hard to feel better from the bite. Pretty soon he walks away, peeks behind himself and sees his tail following him and moving like a snake. I betcha he can't stand it and—oh my goodness, there he goes again trying to get it.

Tommy and I roll on the floor laughing like crazy kids. We see Uncle Carl and Grandma peek around the corner. I am so thankful when they chuckle even if it's just so Auntie will not see what is going on. The half-hour spent with Ted Bear is such a good time that waves of happiness roll over me. I'm having so much fun that I can hardly stand it. A little while ago I was hungry, but now when I'm called to supper, it's just taking away my time to play with Ted Bear. Could it be that it was not food I needed but something to make me laugh and forget my misery? This is the first time since Mama left that I have forgotten about how sad I am. Even if it's only for a little while, the joy I feel helps to make the bad things go away.

I thank God for this joy. I would like to ask Him for a little more, but I am careful not to ask for too much. After dinner and now feeling new hope, I pet the dear little cat before he continues his run-after-his-tail races. I even smile a little, surprising even myself.

If only Mama could be here to watch this. Oh, there I go again wishing she was here and, as always, wondering what she's doing. It happens day after day, time and time again.

Chapter 5

Sizzling Heat

Jenny

For hours, I've been lying awake with my eyes closed as I practice for an interview I don't yet have, but that ends when I hear the tapping of little feet and see a tiny figure standing at the foot of my bed.

"Good morning, Becky. Are you getting ready to leave on vacation?"

She grins, turns, and runs from the room only to collide with her mother who is turning the corner.

"Oops," Ruth laughs. "Where are you going in such a hurry, young lady? Come, let's say goodbye to Aunt Jenny before we leave." She takes the child's hand, and they walk toward me.

"Cliff said we'd better get an early start for Madison before it gets too hot, but I'm so anxious to get to the lodge that he certainly doesn't have to push. Becky, can you give Aunt Jenny a kiss goodbye?"

Filled with excitement and mischief, Becky raises her arm and proceeds to open and shut her tiny fist before running once again from the room. Almost immediately, she peeks around the corner only to return and plant a wet kiss on my cheek. Ruth and I smile at her gestures.

"Goodbye, sweetheart," I call. "Have a good time, and be sure to take good care of Mommy and Daddy."

"Help yourself to anything you need, dear," Ruth calls to me. "There's plenty of milk, butter, bread, rolls, and leftovers in the icebox."

For a short while, the ruckus of completing last-minute tasks continues until I hear the door close and the apartment is converted to alarming tranquility. It soothes me into sleeping once again.

I gasp for air and then twist my head to the left and blink my eyes. For a time, I cannot recall where I am until I remember this is Ruth and Cliff's apartment. I'm sprawled out on the kitchen floor, so conceivably, I fainted. I do not recall that or anything else, so what could have happened? Had I come into this room for something to eat? My hand aches as I reach to wipe my forehead and then am astounded to find I am wearing nothing but perspiration.

A horrible thought emerges that cousin Ruth or Cliff might burst in and find me like this. I panic until I remember they are vacationing with Ruth's mother and sister Dolores. Had they not been, could I have put on so much as panties or a slip? Any clothing would have stuck to me like cement.

With the help of a table leg, I pull myself to a sitting position and notice the newspaper on the chair next to me. The headlines read: TEMPERATURES REACH 106 AND PUT MANY IN LOCAL HOSPITALS. The story continues with, "Heat restricts activities while folks sleep in parks to escape their stifling residences."

I crawl to the window and witness countless folks spread out on the grass in the park across the street. If I had not been so fearful I might have joined them, but I am aware that if anything happens to me that there would be no one to notify my family, and that thought is terrifying.

"Darn you, Jonathan," I wail. "You made a mess of our lives so instead of the happy family that lived in Laurel Hill a little over a year ago, we're separated so all that remains is pain." I utter a cry of rage and begin to howl like a tormented puppy until tears run down my cheeks and drop to mix with beads of sweat.

Another day of heat. I venture into the kitchen to run tap water that naturally is warm, so I open the top of the icebox to chip off a chunk of ice to add to the water. It's melting fast. I'm not fond of water but crave it now and drink too hastily. A painful lump in my chest stops me and, with a moan, I remember to drink slowly when I'm at this point of dehydration.

A burp relieves the pressure, and I reopen the icebox to find nothing appeals to me. Water will have to suffice for now, and that might not be bad since I know it will keep one alive longer than food.

I limp to the bathroom with its decorative tub and claw feet to fill it again with what proves to be lukewarm water. It's now so full that there is barely room for my body to slip in without the water flowing over the edge. I lean against the back of the tub and close my eyes. Want ads flash before my eyes, and I know I should be applying for jobs listed in the newspaper, especially one in particular that interests me. But it is yet too hot to get dressed and leave for that interview. If this heat doesn't let up by tomorrow, I'll have to try to get dressed despite my appearance. I certainly hope someone offering a job has this new thing called air-conditioning so we won't suffer the way we do now.

I'm not only frustrated but downcast; maybe because I am alone and there is no one to talk to. My problem is that when I'm isolated I have a tendency to think about myself too much, which is what I am doing right now. I have not earned enough money for any of this to be worthwhile, and my concern is that I will not be able to continue my life insurance payments so the children will be protected.

By now, my family in Duluth is no doubt wondering if something has happened to me since they know Ruth and her family are on vacation. Maybe I can put on enough clothes to pick up the mail and learn if there is news from them before I try to write. Jonathan has not written to explain why he has been sentenced to spend time in Illinois, so his punishment must be severe. This keeps torturing me.

Although I was certain my husband would allow me to attend the interrogation in Sault Sainte Marie, Jon just glared at me with his steely eyes and ordered me to sit on the bench outside the courtroom. He warned me not to try to sneak in to listen to the proceedings as that would truly upset him.

Gut-wrenching fear made me do what he asked. Why did I fear him when I wasn't afraid of other men? That terror seems to be a web that has held me hostage since I married this man who is twelve years my senior. He became an even more forceful person after he was successful in his role at the bank, and I definitely noticed a change in him when he was made a member of the board. Then he took on an even more authoritative attitude.

To me, a century passed until the trial hearing was over, and I caught myself wringing my hands as I paced the floor. The longer I waited, the more fearful and upset I became. When cousin George eventually came out to tell me my husband had been sentenced to an Illinois correction center, I felt as if all my strength had been drained. But what he said next was worse.

He told me that Jonathan raised his voice as they were about to leave the courtroom and said, "Let's get this over with, and take me to Illinois as soon as you can. I can't leave here fast enough."

Didn't he ask to see me?

"I'm truly sorry, my dear, but he didn't. I have no idea why except that he was most troubled."

Jonathan could not have hurt me more. What did cousin George think? I was too humiliated to ask him what went on during the trial and could not even bring up the subject. I knew nothing about why he was being punished. Should not a wife know these things about her husband? What was I to Jonathan, woman or child?

Before we arrived in Duluth, I asked George the name of Jon's lawyer. I told him we were introduced before he entered the courtroom, so I understand he is from Laurel Hill but can't recall his name. Paul something?

"Paul Baranger," George answered. "He did an excellent job but was not able to get the sentence reduced at this time. We made a bargain to meet soon and prepare plans to see what we can do for Jonathan."

Dear George. If anyone can help, he can. I remember his encouraging eyes and that interesting mustache. Usually I don't like hair on a man's face, but with George, it's a sign of dignity. He might be Jonathan's cousin but is truly a cousin to both of us.

Enough of this. Now I must see if I can get to that mailbox and find out if Maggie is all right. I'm sure she's heard I'm alone this week and could be concerned about me.

Chapter 6

Why Did I Marry Him?

Jenny

"Why don't we change into our nightgowns, robes, and slippers," Ruth calls from her bedroom. "That way, we can be more comfortable and just hop into bed when we're tired."

"Good idea, cuz."

Cliff is at another evening lodge meeting, and Becky has been tucked into bed. Ruth tells me about her relaxing vacation and how good it was to see her mother and sister. I ask many questions about her mother because Bertina has always been one of my favorites. Ruth informs me her sister Dolores is doing great and appreciated the vacation.

My story is not a joyful one, but I seem to keep Ruth on edge as I describe my latest experience. I tell her about the killing heat we had here in town while she and her family were cooling off at the lake. "But now I must tell you about something more important.

"Much to my dismay, the temperature didn't drop for many days, but when I managed to put on my clothes and the perspiration didn't run down my face so I looked as if I were crying, I scheduled an interview with a doctor who cares for patients of many wealthy families. Unfortunately one of the job openings that interested me had been filled."

Ruth looks disappointed, so I hurry on because good news follows. "But, Ruth, the other job was still open." Now she smiles as if relieved.

"The doctor said that if he's satisfied with a promising candidate for the job, the family has given him the power to hire. Mrs. Granger and her newborn baby girl are due home from the hospital this coming week, and to date, he hadn't found a suitable candidate for her so he's continuing his interviews.

"Ruth, Dr. Sutherland and I had a most favorable interview. He said this job is mine if I want it and also asked me to contact him when the two months is up to see if he has another assignment for me. I thanked him for his understanding of how much I love children and for his faith in my ability to handle this job."

"Does it pay enough to satisfy your needs, Jenny?"

"Yes, this first one does, and hopefully with the experience of this assignment, I'll be offered at least an equal amount for my next job.

"Tell me more," Ruth says.

"My only duty will be caring for the mother and baby. I start work in two days and will live on the premises except for one day off a week."

Keep the majority of your clothes here," Ruth suggests. "You're most welcome to the room you have now, and if we can spend some time together on your free day, it will be special for both of us." I tell her I am most thankful and sigh with relief.

We had intended to have but a light conversation, but now I feel as if I'm being nudged by some unseen being to relate some of my deepest feelings since we seldom have this special time to chat without Cliff or Becky interrupting. To date, I haven't shared any of my difficult times with anyone, and how special it will be to review my past with Ruth. My thoughts, at least in the beginning, roll out like I'm trying to escape an approaching tornado.

"You didn't love him? You actually married Jonathan when you didn't love him?" Ruth stares at me as if I've announced the moon has plummeted into the park next door. "Whatever made you do it?" she asks. Feeling stupid, I begin to wonder if I should have even begun this revelation though I had to tell someone soon. Who better than Ruth?

"I wish I really knew why, but since I'm still trying to sort this out myself, perhaps I should try another approach. You know how some people believe accepting a ring is almost as sacred as getting married. Unfortunately I'm one of them. Jonathan proposed and even though at first I hesitated to give him an answer, I finally said *yes* and accepted his ring. Unknown even to me, the damage was already done as I now considered myself pledged to Jon. Some people believe it's okay to agree to marriage before you're sure, but I've learned it isn't smart or healthy because as time passed I wondered if I ever really loved Jonathan."

I take another sip of coffee while continuing to sort out my feelings, and the room falls silent. Ruth is patient and continues mending Becky's dress to fill in the quiet time. Finally, I'm able to continue.

"Jon is nice-looking and still has a handsome physique even though he's twelve years older than I am. I found he certainly is persuasive. Perhaps I agreed to marry him because he portrayed himself as one type of person when he is actually someone else."

Ruth seems puzzled. "I'm sorry, but I don't follow you."

"Maybe it would be best if I gave you an example. Without consulting me, Jonathan purchased season tickets to the Orpheum Theater in two of the best seats in the house, seventh row center, so we could see all the vaudeville shows. I was spellbound with appearances by Eddie Cantor, George Burns, and other well-known entertainers and convinced myself Jonathan truly enjoyed this type of entertainment. I'm sure you know, Ruth, how much I adore vaudeville. I don't remember mentioning that to Jonathan and unfortunately assumed we have the same interests. I couldn't have been more wrong and learned later that this was his way of impressing me and making sure I'd go through with our plans to marry. After we were married, I discovered he was an avid sports fan, which he never told me during the courtship perhaps because I mentioned once that I didn't enjoy sports. What puzzles me is why was it so difficult to be honest?"

"If you had doubts that this was not the husband for you, why didn't you call it off? Couldn't you see how much better that would have been?" Ruth looks at me as if I've lost my mind. She could be right since how can I get her to understand when I don't myself? I fidget and make another attempt.

"Let me put it this way. Jon lost his job shortly after he gave me the ring, and that only added to my worries. What would people think of me if I broke off our engagement when the man had no job? That would be cruel. Would others believe I would only marry Jon to be supported—many women do that, you know. Yet others might wonder how I could marry someone who didn't have a job to support me as folks have been known to believe such conduct is ludicrous. After about a year of tossing those thoughts around, I knew I'd better either marry Jonathan or give back his ring and enjoy freedom once again."

"You just said 'enjoy freedom.' Doesn't that tell you something, Jenny? If being engaged to Jonathan wasn't making you happy, how could you expect marriage would be any better?"

Does Ruth understand any of this? There's no turning back so if I made a mistake in bringing this up tonight; it's too late now.

"Ruth, all the time I was trying to decide what to do, Jon kept harassing me to get married. Finally I gave in and we eloped."

Surprise must have caused her to slap her hand on the table, and I jumped. Apparently, I'd hit a bombshell.

"Did you really say you eloped?" Ruth asks. "You who always wanted a fancy wedding and *you* eloped? For heaven sakes, where did you go?"

"It wasn't too difficult. Jonathan has a cousin and his wife on the iron range, and we once visited them. We told anyone who asked us where we were headed that we were going to visit the Murphys, but we didn't actually do that but went to a nearby town. Prior to the wedding, Jonathan borrowed Jake's car to drive to Hibbing to obtain our marriage license, so we were now assured that it would not appear in the Duluth paper and no one would know. I didn't even tell Mother or my sisters."

It is funny, I think to myself, *that now that I'm discussing this, it actually does sound irrational.*

"If only you hadn't lived in southern Minnesota at that time so we could have discussed this. You might have helped me come to my senses, Ruth, because I most certainly needed someone I could talk to before I took this leap into disaster. You and I were both so totally caught up in our own lives that we hadn't communicated even by mail, and for that, I take responsibility since I was never much of a letter writer. Now I truly regret it."

Abruptly I think of something so amusing that I grin and cry out, "If what I've told you already seems strange, what do you think of this? We didn't even have intercourse for four months after I became Mrs. Westin."

"Now I've heard it all," Ruth says as she rises to pour another cup of coffee. When she reaches the stove she puts down the cup and murmurs mainly to herself, "No, this won't do it." I watch her fumble in an upper cupboard and shove a few things around until she finds a bottle; then she reaches for two small glasses.

"This bootleg whiskey is potent stuff," Ruth tells me as she pours a small amount in each glass and adds water and chunks of ice. "You have the day off tomorrow, Jenny, so why not try it. You seem so tense, and this might relax you. I know it will certainly relax me," she says as she lifts our glasses and walks toward me. She puts one in front of me and the other at her place before sitting down.

"Try this, Jenny, and then back to your story that so far makes little or no sense. How in heaven's name did you get by without having sex for four months? By this time, I'm convinced you want nothing to do with that three-letter word."

"It's not that, Ruth, but no one knew we were married." I sense this is getting more difficult to relate, so I take one swallow of the drink and must have made a face because Ruth grins.

"It gets better as you drink it," she assures me.

"Ruth, it was and still is a strange marriage. When we returned to Duluth, I went back to Mother's house and Jonathan continued to stay with his sister Alma and her husband where he'd been living since he lost his job. He had no car, so we had little time alone."

"Wait a minute," Ruth says. "Haven't you forgotten something? If you went up on the range under the pretext you were visiting the Murphys, how about the wedding night when you went to some other range town instead?"

"Hibbing."

"Immaterial."

I sip from the small glass in front of me and begin to cough. I've seldom had liquor and then nothing stronger than homemade wine. This bootleg liquor is far more repulsive to me, but not wanting to offend Ruth or appear unsophisticated, I continue to sip the nasty stuff even if it's making me feel strange. Before long, a warm feeling begins to flow through my veins and I feel tingly, not even aware that Ruth is quietly studying me.

"Well, we were married by the justice of the peace and then went to get something to eat. Before we finished eating, I thought of something important that wasn't easy to discuss, but I had to wait until I got up the nerve to talk about it. We hadn't discussed birth control.

When I mentioned this to Jon, he stared at me and said, 'We don't need any protection, Jenny. That would only take away the pleasure of the experience. After all, we *are* married.'"

I stop my tale momentarily and lean back in my chair. Whoops, my tummy is beginning to hurt a little. *Burp*. Oh, that's better. How strange that now I feel like sharing this with the whole world no matter how insane it might sound.

"Ruth, do you remember when I learned how babies were born? I wouldn't date anyone for weeks because that was the most unspeakable thing I'd ever heard. Do you know that on my wedding night it scared me half to death to think I might get pregnant when I wasn't even ready to tell anyone I was married?"

Ruth sits back and shakes her head. "Well, I might as well hear this too. How did you handle that one?" My enthusiasm rises as now I've shared so much with Ruth that I'm only too anxious to tell what happened.

"First, I went into the bathroom to undress, and I just took my little old sweet time lingering in there before coming out. Then I stood at the mirror with my robe tied tightly around me, took down my hair, and brushed it a long time to delay things while I spoke ever so softly to keep up a conversation. I was relieved when I realized it was working and that Jonathan was getting drowsy.

"Did you know, Ruth, that he was brought up on a farm and never broke the habit of getting up early and hitting the old bed right after sundown?"

"Yes, Jenny, you told me."

"Oh." Things in the room are beginning to spin a little, and I grin before shaking my head and pointing my finger at Ruth to say, "Can you imagine how relieved I was when I heard his heavy breathing and snoring and realized he had fallen asleep?"

"As long as you're talking about yourself instead of me, then I can," says Ruth.

"What do you mean by that?"

"Well, I always wanted sex on my wedding night."

"But I hadn't even told anyone I was getting married, and if I got pregnant I would be in deep trouble because someone might think I did that thing before I got married."

"Okay, so I suppose I understand," Ruth says as she tells me to continue my story.

"The next morning I did a good job of pretending I had 'a visitor,' and he wasn't about to mess with that."

Ruth looks at me with a funny expression on her face before saying, "Now who isn't being honest?"

Oh dear, she's right. To cover my embarrassment I move on.

"I was safe for four months until the weekend Jon's sister Alma and her husband, Jake, went to visit Aunt Ida on the farm to spend a couple days with her relatives."

"Ah hah! I see where this is going," Ruth says.

"Yup. Jonathan called that very day and said we could now be alone. He urged me to hurry as fast as I can to get a streetcar. I panicked." Oops, I think the room must be spinning a little, but maybe that's just my imagination.

"It's like this," I continue. "I told him I felt ill. He assured me he'd take good care of me. I told him I should wash up. He said he'd run a hot bath for me. "I'm hungry, I told him. He said he'd fix me a nice steak and then I'd feel better."

I grimace and study Ruth before saying, "I might as well admit I gave in because I actually didn't know how to get out of it." *There. I finally got that out.*

A hiccup makes me giggle before I tell Ruth, "Oh, I was so horribly immature and not quite with it yet." In an attempt to gain control over my persistent and annoying hiccups, I saunter to the sink for a glass of water and drink slowly while trying to hold my breath. When that's over, I turn and struggle to control my feet that do not seem to know their way back to the chair where I was sitting. Stupid feet.

Momentarily I gain my poise. "It was lucky we didn't have sex on our wedding night because that night with Jon at Alma's house was my first experience with intercourse. I got pregnant with Maggie right away." I swing my hand in front of her. "Fast like a bunny, that little ole secret could no longer be a secret."

"I think we'd better get you to bed, Jenny," Ruth says. "The whiskey isn't doing good things for you. Aren't you used to liquor?"

"No, but I feel *swell*. And wait, 'cause I've got to tell you the rest of the story because there's good news too." I draw a big breath. "Soon after that, Jonathan got a job as bookkeeper at some little ole furniture store in West End. Some Scandinavian name like—oh, what was it?" I feel myself struggling to get the name right. "Oh ya. Now I remember. It was Johnsons." My intelligence makes me beam, but the grin soon collapses. "No, it was Andersons. Anderson's Furniture Store. When Jonathan knew for sure he had the job, I announced our marriage to my family. Hic."

I follow her into the bedroom and moan. "Oh, Ruth, I don't feel so good."

Chapter 7

Waiting for the Mail

Maggie

Tommy's room is so small that there's only space for his small bed and dresser. It has only one window, but I'm happy it faces the street where I can kneel and watch for the mailman. Today I've been extra anxious and have been paying close attention to the clock. I just know he will bring the mail any minute now. In this morning's delivery, there was nothing from Mama, so I certainly hope a letter comes this afternoon.

If only we had a telephone so I could talk to her, but Auntie Marie says we can't afford luxuries like that. Even if we could, she told me it would cost too much to call long distance so I suppose a telephone wouldn't help me anyway. I need so bad to tell Mama how I wait day after day for the mail just hoping there will be a letter from her. I'm doing too much anxious waiting that makes me tense, or at least, that's what Auntie Marie has been teaching me.

Maybe something has happened to Mama. She was supposed to be alone last week when Auntie Ruth and her family went to some lodge. Now that really sends shivers up and down me. If something bad has happened to Mama, who would help her?

I must stop thinking like that, or I'll go crazy. While I'm waiting, I suppose I could open my tablet and get my pencil ready to write a letter to her, but what would I say? I don't want to upset her like telling Mama how unhappy I am here. If only I knew when she could visit us, which would be so wonderful because even though Uncle Carl and Grandma are nice to me, Auntie Marie is so different from Mama. She's hard to get used to because she has all these rules, and the one I hate most of all is that now school has begun I have to go to bed at eight o'clock. That's dumb.

Mama knows there's a grandfather clock in the kitchen that chimes every hour. When it strikes eight, Auntie Marie's eyes are glued on me even if she doesn't say a word, and then I gotta pack up my schoolbooks and go upstairs. Mama never used to make me go to bed that early. Maybe I should tell her about this so she could talk some sense into Auntie Marie.

I can't tell her about how lonely I am because I never felt lonesome or scared when I was with her. There aren't any children in this neighborhood to play with, so most of the time, I play with Tommy or stay indoors by myself. Auntie Marie thinks it's enough to have Tommy for company, but he's such a pesty little kid and never wants to play anything I like.

I could tell Mama about school. It would be okay if I had been here from the time I was little because then I would be like the other kids and have a special playmate. Some of them have known each other since kindergarten like I knew Marilyn in Laurel Hill. I only gotta go across the street to school now, but I used to like walking with my friend when we hiked two miles to school. We laughed and talked all the time, and before we knew it, there we were at school. Guess I can't write about that either or she will know how much I miss Laurel Hill. There is one girl here, though, whose name is Elaine Swanson, and she's been very friendly to me. Maybe there's still hope after all, but I can write to Mama about her next time.

One thing I can say is how I try to get the best grades I can in school, but fourth grade is hard. With all those strange kids and a new teacher, I feel so scared when I'm called on to answer a question that my voice just disappears and I have trouble finding it again. I never used to feel that way. What is happening to me?

One good thing, though, is that Miss Jennings reads a chapter from the book *Honeybunch* first thing every morning after we pledge allegiance to the flag. I can hardly wait to get to school, at least for the reading of the next chapter. When she finishes this book, she says she has many other *Honeybunch* books to read to us. I guess I can write about the beginning of our school day 'cause it's so swell.

I pick up my pencil and work fast. Mr. Duffy is coming to our school soon to teach us penmanship. When I look at my scribbling, I can certainly see he's needed. I can tell her that.

I go back to Tommy's window to continue my search for the mailman who certainly must have a letter for me today. Guess that isn't quite yet though because I still don't see him.

There are jobs I have to do every day for Auntie and Grandma. In Laurel Hill, we had Annie and Tinie to clean and take care of us kids. But we don't have them here, so I wonder if they would like to come to Duluth to live? They could do my chores.

Another job I have to do is take care of Tommy. Boy, did I hate doing that at first because it was like I had traded him for my little brother David. Tommy is only four years old so he can't go across the street to my school until next year, and that makes him jealous of me 'cause I can go and he has to stay here.

Last week, Tommy did a good thing though. I can tell Mama about that, so I pick up my pencil again. He talked Auntie Marie into letting the little stray cat that begged at our door into the house. I saw the cat first, and when that little animal looked up at me with those sad blue eyes and let out a tiny meow, I just wanted so bad to open the door and let him in. He is still a little cat; well, kind of small. Auntie said if someone comes for Ted Bear that we must give him back to his real owners. So far no one has come for him, and we're really lucky because it would break my heart into little tiny crispy pieces if someone took him away. I'm the one who named him Ted Bear because he reminds me of a cuddly teddy bear, and I sure love to cuddle him.

I write kinda short letters because I got to be careful what I say so I don't make Mama sad. She would be if I told her how much I miss her; unless, of course, she doesn't feel the same way about me that I do about her.

"Here he comes, Auntie Marie," I squeal. "I saw him." I fly down the stairs and almost fall, so it's a good thing I had a railing to grab. I hope no one saw me or knows what Auntie calls me when I stumble because she says I'm clumsy and certainly shouldn't trip over my own feet.

"Is there a letter from Mama? How is she? Did she get another job yet?"

"Good heavens, Maggie, let me look through the mail first," Auntie says. I march into the kitchen a couple steps behind her. My heart beats fast as I watch her pick up a table knife and slit open a letter.

"Yes, this is from your mother, but I refuse to read this aloud unless you climb on that chair and sit quietly." I do as I'm told.

"Dear family," Auntie Marie reads.

"I'm sorry I couldn't write before, but perhaps you heard about the beastly heat in Milwaukee last week. I hope it wasn't as bad where you are. I'm thankful Ruth and her family were on vacation because I was so hot and sticky that I couldn't even get down to pick up the mail. Your letter sat in the mailbox until today.

"When the unusual heat finally cooled so I could get out, I was hired for one of the jobs I was interested in and start working Monday. I'll be caring for a mother and newborn baby girl when they return from the hospital. I'm excited about that.

"Marie, please give Maggie and everyone my love. Tell my little girl I'll write her soon. Being without work for a while has put me back financially, so it looks as if I might not get home until Christmas.

"Know that I'm okay and miss all of you more than I can put into words. Hopefully this nightmare of being apart from my family will soon be over. My love, Jenny."

The words come out slowly, and I feel a big frown fasten itself to my forehead. "Not until Christmas? Golly, that will take forever."

"Maybe not," says Auntie Marie. "I might have an idea because it helped me when I was your age. Every night I'd check off the date on my calendar, and like magic, what I was waiting for came faster with every day that passed." I study her but cannot see how that will help any.

"May I be excused?"

"Certainly. I know it seems a long time now, Maggie, but you'll be surprised how swiftly the time will go if you play the calendar game."

I climb the stairs slowly and head for my room. *My* room? It's only a room I share with Grandma because nothing in this house is mine except my clothes.

I pull the old rocker over to the window. I miss Mama's hugs and when she would read to me every night from my favorite book *Anne of Green Gables*. Now it's on the dresser in the guest room with no one reading it. Mama loves books, so maybe that's why the people in a book come alive when she acts out stories as she reads to me. She asked me not to tell anyone but when she was a little girl she used to read by candlelight for hours while lying in bed until she got too sleepy to go on.

There was no electricity then. Candles are dangerous as they could cause fires, but Mama said she was always very careful.

Christmas used to be waiting for presents. Now it's waiting for Mama.

Chapter 8

A Mansion but Not Mine

Jenny

It's early morning when I cautiously descend the steps. Cliff and Ruth helped me with directions and the streetcar route, and Cliff told me the house would probably be only a block or two north of where I get off the trolley.

A gentle rain fell during the night, and the green grass is saturated with moisture. I shift my heavy suitcase from one hand to the other and wonder why I packed so much, but then how did I know what type of clothes I'd be expected to wear when until now I've never had a job like this. The garments I wore in Upper Michigan are no longer new but clean, striking, and not yet out of style. With our country in this Depression, I'm not sure anyone would notice if they were old because most of us must continue to wear what we have. New stylish clothes are for those who have money to spare and can afford to be fashionable.

The houses I pass are enormous and bordered by ornate iron fences. A boulevard with young trees runs down the center of the wide street. I'm profoundly impressed with this prodigious neighborhood. The buildings date back to an earlier time and are well-preserved and adorned by their well-groomed grounds.

It feels good to breathe deeply to enjoy the freshness of the morning air, and how fortunate I was not scheduled to work the day after my experience with the bootleg liquor. I had awakened that next morning with a pounding headache, and worse yet, I was sick to my stomach and made several trips to the bathroom. No matter how I struggled to get up for the day, my head ached so intensely that I could only lie back and allow the morning to evaporate.

No more of that. At first, I refused to accept Ruth's offer as I did not care for the taste of the illegal whiskey. But as I sipped it, I discovered it was easier to share my pathetic experiences with her though the emotional relief was not worth the price I paid.

When the home I look for comes into view, I check the address to assure that it is the one I seek, and my pace slows. This is an even larger mansion than the gracious home I visited in Duluth when I was sixteen. On that occasion, I accompanied my talented neighbor Robert when he was hired to play his accordion at a small dinner–dance gathering.

He was exceptionally talented. Robert lived but two doors from our house, and I was always delighted when he came to serenade me. I was aware that he had a crush on me so wasn't surprised when he asked me to join him at this gathering in one of Duluth's many wealthy homes.

He had received permission from the lady of the house that I be seated at a small table in a recessed area where he could join me during breaks from his performance. The butler intermittently brought me fancy sandwiches and cakes that truly made me feel like a queen as I quietly tapped my feet to the music. What if I were the wife of a wealthy man who would build a house like this for me? The experience had such an impact that wild dreams sprouted and grew to massive heights. As expected, during intermissions Robert joined me, and I had an opportunity to thank him and express how much I was enjoying the evening although I was careful not to share my wild dreams. He might find those thoughts silly since he was a man, and I doubt they dream such dreams.

But that is all in the past, and now as I stare at this lavish residence and realize I will be but an employee, the realization does not check my fantasies. I stop to study the unusual architecture of this immense brick home. It, too, is surrounded by an elegant iron fence. I can barely make it out but isn't that a greenhouse in the back of the house? Late summer flowers bloom in all areas of the yard, adding spectacular color to the green bushes that already grow there. This is indeed a showplace.

My wavy hair has been disheveled by the wind, so I run my fingers through it before attempting to open the gate. Success! I throw back my shoulders, lift my chin, and move with haste straight ahead. Six cement steps rise to the front entrance, and with renewed confidence, I ring the doorbell.

"Yes?" The woman who answers the bell wrinkles her brow and stares at me. Two small bodies hide behind her skirt and tiny eyes peer inquisitively at me. Someone quickly sweeps them away as if they have been gobbled up by a vacuum cleaner.

I smile as I introduce myself and explain I have been instructed to be present when Mrs. Granger returns from the hospital. The woman introduces herself as Mrs. Gary, the housekeeper, and she explains in a dictatorial manner that all servants must use the back door. Without a doubt that includes me, so I apologize for my error.

"This time, it's acceptable," she says, "but from now on, use that entrance."

"Yes, ma'am," I say respectfully. She has a voice that makes me feel like I'm her child and have just embarrassed her by being sent to the police department for stealing bubble gum.

I'm led by the stern Mrs. Gary to the majestic stairway that rises before us. As we ascend, I glance over the railing to admire the handsome foyer and catch a glimpse of a portion of the living room with its magnificent fireplace. The stairway turns before we reach the next level, and I follow the housekeeper down a long hall. We pass two doors before she opens the third access on the right where I observe a spacious room with several windows facing the front of the house.

Soft green drapes are tied back for a better view, and a dresser is on the right side of the bed with a small cradle on the left. The walls are covered with ornately patterned green and white wallpaper whose colors match those found in the bedspread that covers the four-poster bed. A small fireplace is at the opposite end of the room with a door to the right that Mrs. Gary explains connects this room with that of our mistress.

"Are you saying that this is my room? I always thought the help occupied the upper level."

"Well, Miss," answers the lady in charge, "you are one of the more fortunate to have this large, cheerful area because it's adjacent to Mrs. Granger's room. You must be near the lady of the house who will nurse the baby before giving her to you for your care. This room and that of Mrs. Granger's connect with the master's chamber."

Mrs. Gary abruptly changes the subject. She informs me that I will be called for lunch momentarily, then closes the door quietly as if to demonstrate how this must be done. I open the large wardrobe closet to find it empty, so I hang my dresses therein before opening drawers to lay out my freshly laundered undergarments. I change into a plain white blouse and black skirt after which there seems nothing further to do but wait to be called for the noon meal.

If my dreams included being served in the dining room, the assumption quickly disappears when I am escorted by a servant to the kitchen where I join other staff members at a lengthy table and pull out a vacant chair. The woman on my right introduces herself as Marian and tells me she has charge of the little ones in the family.

"Normally I eat with them," she enlightens me, "but today the children's reading instructor is in charge for the next hour."

I'm famished and am thankful for the peaches and cottage cheese salad and the tasty egg sandwiches, but when those dishes are removed and the cook brings in coffee and two plates of frosted chocolate cookies to be passed, I'm convinced after one bite that the woman is a great chef. Anyone who excels at baking has to be.

The staff seems agreeable and small talk helps the time pass quickly. I feel a sense of nervous excitement as Mrs. Granger's arrival approaches, so I'm grateful when Marion invites me to meet the youngsters who are in her care. Three-year-old Helen is fair with blond hair and possesses a sparkling personality. Two-year-old Michael is handsome and shy, but it's one-year-old Matthew who steals my heart. I lift the tiny child into my arms and tickle him tenderly before I whisper in his ear and gently rub his back. By now, I'm convinced I will truly enjoy my stay in this home.

It is shortly after 2:00 PM when Mrs. Granger arrives with the new baby, and I stand by ready to greet her. A powerful breeze blows into the room as the door opens, and the chauffeur quickly closes it behind the young and attractive Mrs. Granger. She views me with an inquisitive look until we are introduced and then smiles and says as she hands me the infant, "This is Sarah."

I hold the newborn delicately and study the blue eyes and tiny face. What a beautiful baby you are and how fortunate to be raised in this handsome home with so many servants. Your mother will have ample time to enjoy you.

My orientation to Sarah's comfort and where her needs are to be kept causes the day to pass quickly. A servant brings the evening meal to my room while Sarah is sleeping after which I realize that I'm exhausted. It's been a long day but an exciting and happy one.

As the darkness of evening closes in, I wearily burp and diaper the baby after she has been breast-fed by her mother.

I gently place Sarah in the cradle next to my bed, then rock it slowly until the newest family member dozes off. That's it, I conclude, at least until she awakens with further needs. I quickly put on my nightgown and sink into the soft mattress where I fall asleep within minutes.

How long I rest I don't know but am awakened by a cry and quick running footsteps. The door that connects our rooms opens and shuts noisily as if the person has forgotten about the sleeping baby, and I'm thankful there is a soft light in the room so I can confirm it is my mistress. Next I hear a moan from the crib that accelerates until the baby bellows, so I quickly lift Sarah into my arms until she is consoled and settles down. When I am sure it is safe to return to my bed, I'm astonished to find Mrs. Granger has already settled in.

"Please help me," the woman pleads, "because I need to sleep here tonight. I'm sure this is embarrassing to you and certainly an inconvenience, Jenny, but I beg of you not to force me to return to that room." I notice her body is quivering under the blanket.

"What seems to be the trouble?"

The frail woman doesn't answer for some time. At length, she snaps, "That most certainly is private!"

As we both lie awake for what seems hours, tossing until the sheets are pulled from the bottom of the bed, Mrs. Granger sighs and says, "I suppose I must talk to someone, and though I barely know you, you're the candidate since you're the only one here." She catches her breath and appears to be struggling to gain control. When she speaks again, her voice sounds raspy and low as if her teeth are clenched.

"This happens every time I give birth and return home from the hospital. He tries to force himself on me, and when he's sure I won't give in, he rapes me. The pain is unbearable so soon after giving birth, and I hate it. He did not stop me tonight because I made a fuss and headed for your room, but there will be many other nights—horrible nights. I'm not ready for that yet," she tells me as she sobs bitterly and hides her face in the pillow.

Embarrassed by all these personal issues being shared with me, I creep out of bed in the semidarkness, straighten the sheets best I can, and tuck them in again. The emotional conversation and sound of crying must have awakened and disturbed Sarah, so I take her in my arms to reassure her. Mrs. Granger motions that I hand her the baby as she feels that feeding might calm her. When that is accomplished, I go through the burping and cradle rocking again. When Sarah is quiet, I cover the distraught woman and remain awake until she falls asleep.

What have I got myself into now? How foolish and wrong I have been all these years to believe that because people have an enormous amount of money and a handsome home that they have no problems. Will I be able to tolerate the pressure of being caught in the middle of such personal unhappiness for the next two months? Right now I wonder.

Chapter 9

The Speakeasy

Jenny

Energetically I climb the familiar wooden steps leading to Ruth and Cliff's apartment, but my mind is still on the mansion. Thankfully Mrs. Granger didn't storm into my room again as she had on that loathsome night when she announced she could not return to her own room. I heard whimpering and pleading drifting from my mistress's room several evenings later that ceased when the door to the master bedroom slammed shut. Sporadically there would be a muffled scream that caused me to cover my ears although I knew I could do nothing to help. No staff member dares to interfere with our employer's personal problems—certainly not me since I desperately need this job.

How very welcome is Ruth's embrace, and I sink into a kitchen chair to stretch out my legs and enjoy the coffee she sets before me. Ruth cheerfully announces that breakfast will soon be ready.

"Hi, Aunt Yenny," a soft voice beckons from the doorway. The child's head tilts shyly and stays there as her eyes slowly rise to meet mine. I sit up straight as I know what is coming. As if gunned by pushing an accelerator, Becky's feet race across the room to propel herself into my arms. I sweep the child onto my lap to hug and kiss her before asking what she has been doing while I was away. The story is longer than I had anticipated, but when she catches her breath, I grin as she tells me, "But I was still lonesome for you."

Becky departs to play in the next room, and an enticing whiff reaches my nostrils as Ruth hands me a plate of crisp bacon, eggs, toast, and jam.

"Thanks, Ruth. This looks so good, and I'm famished." Within moments of satisfying bites, the conversation reaches a crescendo when I relate the goings-on in the wealthy home.

"So it was an eye-opener? You had no idea something like this goes on?" Ruth asks as she studies me.

I hate to admit it because under the scrutiny of her expression I suddenly feel very immature. Ruth extends her right hand for emphasis as she explains, "Wealthy men have tremendous influence, and they can twist the truth to make their wives appear as if they were at fault. There's a grave threat she may lose her children. Most of these women have little choice but to grin and bear it."

"I'm beginning to believe it's no great blessing to be married to a rich man."

Ruth nods in agreement before proceeding to the kitchen cabinets to retrieve two letters.

"These came for you," she announces as she hands them to me.

When I see my sister Marie's familiar handwriting, I smile because it will be good to learn how everything is in Duluth. Before I open it, though, I glance at the other dispatch. The handwriting is not familiar, but I do recognize the name on the return address.

"This letter, Ruth, is from Jonathan's attorney. Recently I received a note from him asking me to meet with him when he is in Milwaukee on business, so I informed him I had Fridays free. Let's see what he says," I say as I rip open the envelope.

Ruth slowly clears the table as if waiting to see if I have anything further to share. She does not have to wait long as the letter is short.

"He says he would like to pick me up at your apartment to take me to dinner a week from today. I suppose that's not a problem. Do you think he'll give me some idea as to why Jon has been sentenced for a crime?"

"The only way you're going to know is if you meet with him." Ruth sits down again. "How did he know where to reach you?"

"He called at Mother's house, and when he didn't find me there, Marie gave him your address."

"I'm just glad it isn't tonight because Cliff and I want to take you to a speakeasy. It's about time you're exposed to some of what goes on in this world."

"Do they have anything but that bootleg whiskey? I don't want to drink that horrible stuff again."

"You'll get over that hangover one of these days, Jenny. That's the only beverage they serve in this place. Maybe it's best to try it again soon. How about ordering a glass and taking a few sips as I'm sure Cliff will be happy to help you finish it."

"Ruth, I'll be glad to join you and Cliff." Thanks for the invitation." My eyes fall back to the letter. I certainly wish I knew why Jon's lawyer wants to see me."

Ruth takes the rest of the dishes to the sink and throws a bar of Ivory soap into the dishpan before filling it with hot water.

I open the letter from Marie and smile. And here's a note from Maggie to make this day special.

"I thought we were going to a . . ." but I stop when I feel the nudge that Ruth gives me. "What was it you needed?" she asks as she turns me into an aisle where we are alone but surrounded by health aides and toothpaste. She lifts her finger to her lips. "Shhhh," she whispers. "Don't say another word but pretend you're looking for something."

Did Ruth fail to warn me before leaving the apartment that there was a need for caution? It's certainly possible, so I obey without hesitation. I follow her lead and slip behind the counter into another room in the back of the store where we join Cliff. He closes the door quietly behind us and leads us down the hall to yet another room where he presents a card to an attendant. Ruth and I peek in and hear glasses clinking and people laughing as they sit around tables listening to music on a phonograph near the makeshift bar.

"Sorry I forgot to warn you, Jenny," Ruth says. Cliff smiles and escorts us to a table before telling me, "This is what they call a makeshift speakeasy."

"In the back of a drug store?"

"You find them in different places in town. If you have enough money to pay off the right people, you can get by with it." He pulls out a chair for me and asks what I would like to drink.

"You know better than I do, Cliff. Remember that I'm not a drinking woman."

Ruth grins and assures me I am being a good sport before she reiterates, "After living in the big city, we could never send you back to Duluth without completing your education."

Cliff returns with the three glasses of whiskey mixed with water and ice and puts one in front of me. Questioningly I look up at him.

"Did Ruth tell you I'm only going to drink a few sips of this and you are to help me finish it?" I speak hesitantly and probably sound like a child begging for a lifeline.

"She did, but first, let's give it a test. Maybe you'll like this better than what you had at our place."

After a couple sips, I have to admit it is somewhat tastier than the drink I disliked the other night. But I warn them that I am still refusing to swallow much of it. The remembrance of my illness the next morning from guzzling that potent bootleg whiskey is still too keen in my mind. I drink extraordinarily slow until Cliff asks for my attention.

Resembling a college professor, he throws back his shoulders and begins his lecture. "This will help you, Jenny. Allow me to give you a little history.

"The Eighteenth Amendment was passed in 1920 making it illegal to sell liquor . . ."

I rest my chin on my hand and gaze at him as attentively as if I were an honor student. Out of the corner of my eye, I see Ruth grinning. Her husband explains how difficult this amendment has been to enforce because of a lack of adequate police protection.

I see Cliff finds joy in explaining that doctors prescribed it for medicinal purposes like stomach cramps and insomnia. It's obvious he enjoys relating facts he's more knowledgeable about than others present even if the subject is liquor. I conclude Cliff has missed his calling. Then he relates a serious pitfall in this law, and my ears perk-up.

"There's danger too," he continues. "A few years ago, agents raided numerous speakeasies in New York because people were dying from poisonous liquor."

I gulp. "Dying?" I put down my glass with a thud. "Why do people drink this stuff, Cliff?" I push the glass away. "Where does it come from?"

"I didn't mean to unnerve you, Jenny, because there's no need to be concerned in this place. Nationwide, liquor comes from more illegal sources than I care to mention. But I assure you that no one has had any problems here."

"Not yet," I add. But I tell myself that I have certainly lost my taste for what is in my glass.

"I have another announcement to make, ladies. Today I was promoted to assistant manager of our Sears furniture department."

There's a slight pause until Ruth bursts out, "Oh, Cliff, I'm so proud of you. You've worked such a short time in that department and already they've made you an assistant manager."

I am so happy for them that without hesitation I add, "I'm not actually surprised, Cliff. With your personality and intelligence, you're going far."

"Does a salary raise go with it?" Ruth asks.

Cliff looks at her and with a grin shakes his head. "Just like a woman," he says. "Yes, my dear. We might get out of that apartment into a larger complex one of these days."

How enjoyable it is sitting here tonight visiting with both Cliff and Ruth. Usually Cliff is off to meetings, and we see little of him except at supper. We all dream of the future and finish our drinks. Well, not exactly "finish" for me. Before I learned about the problems in New York, I had consumed about a fourth of my drink. After I digested that knowledge, I shoved my glass over to Cliff to claim.

As we leave the "den of iniquity" by another door and listen while someone secures it behind us, we three lock arms and giggle like youngsters, skip at times, then walk leisurely while swinging from side to side, singing, "I had a little drink about an hour ago, and it went right to my head . . ."

If anyone within hearing range witnesses this, I'm sure they know the song applies to the entertainers who are "into their cups" and a "bit" off key.

Chapter 10

Jonathan's Lawyer

Jenny

For work, I wear inexpensive artificial rayon stockings that are most uncomfortable and appear baggy on my legs. Since I'm going out tonight, I tug at my only pair of silk hose while being most careful not to snag them as they are too expensive to replace. After I examine my legs to assure the hosiery seams are straight, I wiggle into a medium-length straight black skirt. My reflection in the mirror assures me that it is not wrinkled, so I slip on an elegant long-sleeved white blouse but see that I need to add color. While searching through my scarves, I find a yellow and green beauty that fits nicely around my neckline. That's better; everything now blends with good taste.

What else do I need? I take a perky black hat out of its box and tip it over my right eye—perfect. The only part of my attire that is worn and a bit shabby is my black fall coat, and I remind myself to remove it quickly when I arrive at the restaurant. Slipping my gloves into one pocket, I face the mirror and turn around slowly for one last look. I have not been out to dinner in so long that I find this occasion frightening.

"Wow!" Ruth says from the doorway as she raises her shoulders and extends her arms showing the palms. "My deah, you are as zee zay, "mag-nee-fee-sant."

"Don't joke, Ruth. You're sweet for trying to lift my spirits, but you know as well as I do that I'm no great beauty. Did I ever tell you that when I was born with this mop of red hair that my mother thought me so ugly she couldn't believe I was part of her family?"

Ruth chuckles. "Oh, Jenny, many babies come into this world looking anything but attractive. But that was then, and now you're grown. How you manage to keep that small waistline after three children is a mystery to me, and it's sad to see you're the only one who doesn't know how attractive you are. My dear, you have a 'disease' called insecurity. How about a cup of tea while you're waiting for Jon's lawyer?"

I'm definitely jittery about this meeting and gladly accept Ruth's invitation. Will I know what to say to him? Will I have any success in learning something about Jon to soothe my tortured mind? Difficult as it is to delve into memories of those ghastly days when my life was torn to shreds, I must know what I'm facing.

"How was the week?" Ruth asks as she stirs sugar into her tea. "I've been out most of the day so I want to catch up."

"Much the same," I tell her. "I'm anxious for the next two months to pass so I can get another assignment. I've given much thought to reporting this to the doctor who hired me, but what good would that do since he might believe I'm dreaming up this horrible story?" It might even cause me to lose my next job."

I jump when the doorbell rings and glance at my watch. "If that's the lawyer, he's definitely early. I've had but a few sips of my tea."

"I'll get it." Ruth rises from the table and hustles to the door.

When she opens it, we see a man of medium height perhaps in his early thirties. His voice is low and articulate when he announces he is Paul Baranger and is here to escort Mrs. Westin to dinner. "Is she here?"

"Come in," Ruth says. "We're having tea. Would you care to join us?"

"Thank you but no tea although I'd be delighted to sit with you while you finish yours."

As soon as he steps into the room, I remember meeting him briefly in the courthouse corridor. It's no wonder I didn't recall him until now. I was so upset that day that if the president of the United States had been standing next to me, I might have mistaken him for the janitor.

"Ruth is certainly a pleasant woman," Paul says as we descend the narrow steps. I couldn't agree with him more. When we reach the sidewalk, he turns to me. I notice his twinkling brown eyes and thick black hair that is cut short but not so short it disrupts his deep waves. He's not what some might call handsome, but he's certainly pleasant with a smile that warms me.

A gust of wind hits us as we step from the protection of the building, and I press my hat firmly to my head to keep it from embarking on a journey of its own. Even though my coat is worn, I welcome its warmth. Paul opens the door of his car to make it easier for me to slide in. Jonathan was never that thoughtful, but then I have no right to be judgmental.

As we drive through the outskirts of the city, a strange shyness comes over me, and I fear this meeting will be awkward. But as we pull up to the diminutive restaurant on the outskirts of the city, I experience a sense of relief. It's a small and intimate bistro where perhaps when we're settled for dinner I can address the issues that perplex me.

After we're seated at a table decorated with red and white checkered tablecloths and the waitress hands us menus, I'm not surprised to see that Italian dishes dominate the choices. The zesty odor of tomato sauce hangs heavy in the air. Not having been exposed to many Italian dishes, I chose spaghetti and meatballs because what can go wrong with that?

The waitress brings water and hot coffee, and after a few sips, I relax somewhat although I know things won't be better until I question this man. I waste no time.

"Why did you want to see me, Mr. Baranger?"

"Paul, please. May I call you Jenny?" I nod to indicate I'm comfortable with that.

"I see you're a woman who doesn't want a lot of small talk but desires to get right to the point, and that suits me. Your husband, Jenny, is not a man open with his feelings, and I failed to learn why he asked to be taken away so quickly after his sentence. Was that because he was disappointed or even angry that you didn't want to be in the courtroom? Was watching the proceedings too difficult for you?"

Stunned, I stare at him. Did he really ask me if I didn't *want* to be present at the trial? I feel the blood burning in my cheeks as my anger builds.

Paul looks confused and asks, "Did I say something wrong?"

I snap my napkin on the table. "I assure you, Mr. Baranger, that it wasn't *my* choice to stay out of the courtroom." My voice is sharp as I mean it to be, and I deliberately called him Mr. Baranger so there would be no misunderstanding that I was indeed aggravated.

"Let's set this record straight," I say in a spiteful manner. "Be assured it was my husband who insisted that I don't enter the courtroom. He demanded in no uncertain terms that I obey his wishes. If you knew him like I do, you'd understand.

"I paced that floor outside the courtroom and was tormented waiting to hear the verdict. I have no answers because Jon left without telling me." Unaware that my voice has reached a crescendo, I continue. "I felt he wasn't treating me as a wife but a child who either couldn't understand or must be protected."

I pause to reflect on my words, then glance around to see if anyone has noticed my outburst. If somebody had, they'd now returned to their conversations or food. I take another sip of coffee, and our eyes meet again. It's strange that I wish the cup contained something stronger than coffee even if I don't like alcohol. It's obvious Paul is puzzled because now I'm certain Jon has given this man the impression that I didn't want to be in the courtroom. My heart pounds as I realize I've been betrayed so I waste no time apologizing to Paul Baranger for the outburst.

"It's become clear that you had no idea what happened prior to the trial," I say sheepishly. "I'm embarrassed because obviously my anger is with Jon, not you. Forgive me?"

"I'm also sorry," he says. "You're right. I didn't understand. I judged you without hearing your side and that's not like me nor should it be the conclusion of any lawyer. Maybe I sensed I needed to talk to you before taking this further, and I'm glad I did."

I make no comment but instead ask the question I've been longing to find an answer to but afraid to ask. "What crime *did* Paul commit?"

The timing is bad because before he has a chance to respond, the waitress approaches with a bowl of steaming minestrone soup. When she walks back to the kitchen, he asks, "You don't know? Just what has Jonathan told you?"

"Nothing," I tell him. "Absolutely nothing. He would never discuss this with me."

I explain how Jon's cousin George drove us to Sault Sainte Marie for Jon's court date. I learned nothing during that return trip and unfortunately was too embarrassed to question George.

"So you don't know why he was fired from the bank?"

I assure him I don't and also explain my bewilderment when we left Laurel Hill so hastily that I barely had time to say good-bye to my closest friends. Jon was actually cruel, and his temper flared when I brought up the subject.

Tears begin to cloud my eyes before I tell him, "I was terrified and humiliated when my friends in Duluth began asking me questions. 'Why am I in Duluth with only the children, and where is Jonathan?' they'd ask. It was humiliating because aren't married people supposed to share both the good and the bad? People expected me to know everything. Instead I feared my silence indicated I had some part in this—whatever that might be. I could not tolerate it any longer and didn't want to see anyone. I was becoming a recluse and understood that before I broke down completely, I'd better accept my cousin Ruth's invitation to visit her in Milwaukee."

I stare at the tablecloth. When I glance up, my eyes lock with Paul's. Slowly and articulately I repeat the one question to which I must have an answer. "So what crime *did* Jon commit?"

"You must know, Jenny, that I cannot release personal information without Jon's permission, but I can tell you what the newspaper printed. Jon was not guilty of taking money himself or buying stocks in his own name. But since an employee who reported to him was guilty of the crime, as his supervisor your husband was also held responsible. There was a question of whether or not he turned his back when the man collected a substantial sum of money from the vault to play the stock market. That happened two weeks before the market crashed. The employee lost everything and couldn't replace the money."

Paul explained it must have been a difficult year for Jon knowing there was a deficit and the bank examiners were due at any time. He was also held responsible for altering the books for a little over a year. When the fatal day did come, it didn't take the officials long to discover the shortage.

"There were too many 'ifs' in Jon's case, so he was asked to leave," Paul says. "For what was believed to be his part in this felony, the judge sentenced him to serve a term in an Illinois corrections center."

My face is burning hot, and I feel weak. "For how long?"

"He hasn't even told you that?"

"I haven't received one letter from him even though I've written. It's as if he's shut me out of his life, yet to my knowledge, I've done nothing to cause this. Why?"

"I can't answer that, Jenny. Whenever Jonathan and I have talked, he's said nothing about his family. I found that strange, so I had to learn more. Apparently he's angry with himself for being such a fool."

Two sizeable platters of spaghetti and meatballs are set before us with a basket of Italian bread and a tiny bowl of butter. I felt some hunger when the evening began, but I no longer have any desire for food. To be polite, I take small bites of the meatballs and simultaneously wind a few spaghetti strands around my fork.

Once again I repeat my question, "How long did the judge rule Jon must serve?" I wait frantically for a response as if a train is approaching and I can't jump off the rails until I have an answer.

"Five years."

I gasp and drop my fork. "Five years?" My heart pounds. "I have three children to worry about, and you say it will be five years?

"I'm so sorry, Jenny," Paul says as he positions his hand over mine in an attempt to soothe me. "Don't give up hope." There's such empathy in his voice that I draw strength from it but say nothing.

"That's the next reason I wanted to see you," he continues as he withdraws his hand. "I'm working with your husband's cousin George to try to get that sentence reduced. We definitely believe we have an excellent chance for that, and I promise to keep you informed of any progress."

I stare at him. He is convincing, but do I believe him because I want to or because I really believe there is a chance?

The apartment is quiet when I return, and I take little time getting to bed. Much to my dismay, I toss for hours. Jonathan allowed a man who reported to him to steal and did not stop him? I cringe at another thought. Did he have hope of getting some of the profits from those illegal stock market transactions for himself? I do not even want to consider that, but our heated conversation this evening blocks my road to sleep.

It's two hours later, and I'm home but still awake. Thoughts and questions continue to swirl in my mind with no one to hear or answer. It has been so long since I've opened up to anyone. Before this nightmare, I could speak with others but never to Jon. Why?

It's always been that way. I get so hurt when he criticizes me and so terrified when he loses his temper. Like the night in Laurel Hill when on a rare occasion I went with Grace to a movie that Jon didn't care to see. Our helpers, Annie and Tinie, were not home to care for the children so Jonathan agreed to stay with them. I had them ready for bed before I left, but when I returned Jon jumped me because Holly had been fussy.

"What kind of a mother are you to leave your children?" he said with a vengeance.

I could hardly believe that he'd said those words. God only knows I seldom go out at night without him. When I saw that Holly's diaper was soaked and her father allowed her to lie there in that condition, I felt ill. What gave Jonathan the power to make *me* feel guilty?

This past year, he's often worked late. One night when I called him at the bank, he was abrupt. When he got home, he was angry and I can yet hear his words of steel.

"Don't ever call me at work again. You might interrupt something highly important." My problem had been urgent, but again after being berated, I felt like I was the one who had sinned. And since he was working at night, what could have been so important he couldn't speak to me?

Why do I fear him? Is it because he is twelve years older than I am and makes me feel like a child? Or is it because he is always in control—and *that* I find intimidating. We never discuss anything intellectual. He constantly puts me down, making me feel insignificant and inferior, so I hardly dare speak my mind.

Oh, heaven help me. Will sleep never come?

Chapter 11

Maggie's Humiliation

Maggie

Colored leaves tumble from the trees and gather in heaps on the street where I shuffle through them on my way to school. They make a crackling sound when I jump on them, and I giggle with this great fun. But a cold wind blows, and I'm glad now that Grandma urged me to wear my coat because it keeps me warm until I enter my school through the side door.

We're learning new things in geography, which is my honest-to-goodness favorite subject 'cause when I see an interesting picture in my class book, it causes me to dream and my thoughts travel to faraway places. Now class is over and it's almost time to go home, but everything changes when someone enters the room to give Miss Jennings a note. Our teacher reads it and says in a big voice so everyone can hear, "Maggie Westin, Miss Wolf wants to see you in her office." I tremble and sense all eyes are on me as if they know why, but I suppose that's silly. It's just that I'm scared and shamed. On the way down the hall to see Miss Wolf, I'm sure my knees will buckle, and it's even more terrifying when I enter her office. She looks at me as if she's going to pull me to pieces, and I can't imagine how I can be in this much trouble.

She marches me to the girl's washroom and points to "Maggie Westin" written on the walls, mirrors, and even on the bathroom stalls. She must be going to show me what some evil person has done. Instead she frowns and says slowly and in a roaring, mean voice, "Why did you do this, Maggie Westin?"

Me? Is she saying that I did this? Holy smokes, I didn't do nothin'. Why should I do something so awful? I can't get one teeny-weeny word out of my mouth to tell her it wasn't me before she starts telling me what to do. Miss Wolf makes Aunt Marie sound like an angel.

"March to the janitor's closet, get a pail and some soap and rags, and then scrub your name from every spot in this room. Do you understand me? When you finish, call me in to inspect your work."

Her squinty eyes and clenched teeth tell me I had better obey and as fast as I can. I shake with fear, and at the same time, I'm about as mad as I've ever been. What do the kids say? Now I remember and wonder if their parents taught them this because of the big words. "Miss Wolf is not one to be reckoned with." Everyone in the school is scared stiff of her.

But she's still talking. "If it isn't accomplished to my satisfaction, you'll do it again before you leave today. I can't allow anything like this to go on in *my* school."

When she leaves, I want to stamp my feet and scream at the top of my lungs. Then I decide to go home and never come back to school. Or maybe I will just run away. Only the truth is I am too scared to do anything but what she tells me to do.

I wash "Maggie Westin" and scrape "Maggie Westin" and scratch "Maggie Westin" at least a hundred times from the walls, mirrors, and partitions that separate the toilets. With almost my last bit of strength, I stamp my foot in anger because I even hate my name. Maybe I, too, will disappear when the last Maggie Westin written in crayon is scraped away.

But I'm not that fortunate. Instead I'm so tired that I fall into a heap on the floor. Crying hasn't been in my heart at all. Why should I cry just because someone is cruel and unfair to me? But everything swiftly changes, and a single tear rides down my cheek before I bury my head in my lap and sob.

When on my way home, I realize I was sweating so much that I didn't even remember to get my coat that I left hanging in the cloak room. When I reach the front door of Grandma's house, my teeth are clicking together like they're cracking nuts, and I shake from the cold.

Grandma fills the bathtub for me, and I get in and rub soap over my whole body to make sure all my tears, sweat, and the dirty water that ran down my arms while I was scraping my name from the walls and toilet stalls has gone away forever. When soaking to rest a bit, my eyes see my broken and torn fingernails. I quiver with anger.

With my last ounce of energy, I dry myself and put on the clothes Grandma laid out for me. I start down the stairs to thank her when I hear Auntie Marie in the kitchen talking to Grandma Nelly. When she sees me, her first words are, "I want you, Maggie, to stay home from school tomorrow morning while I have a word with your principal."

I tremble because I fear Auntie Marie agrees with Miss Wolf. But the next morning when she returns from her meeting, the rain of grief stops pouring over me. Grandma joins us in the living room to hear my aunt's report as I sit on the edge of my chair.

"It was a pleasure to ask that woman, who is supposed to be smart enough to head the entire school, if she has any reasoning power at all," says Aunt Marie. "Would she like me to bring this matter to the attention of the school board so they know the pain she's caused? 'Tell me why,' I ask Miss Wolf, 'would anyone cover walls with their own name? If someone wanted to cause trouble, they'd write another person's name on the walls, not their own."

I stare at my aunt with my mouth open. My worrying was all for nothing because Auntie Marie believes me. As I study her now with her face so angry, I'm happy I'm not Miss Wolf because Aunt Marie is awfully smart, much smarter than Miss Wolf. That's for sure.

My relief only lasts until I learn Auntie Marie asked for my teacher to join them to give her opinion of me as a student. A sense of absolute defeat comes over me because I am sure a bad report will be next. To my surprise, Auntie Marie looks at me and says, "Maggie, Miss Jennings told us that you are adjusting to a new school faster than she had expected. She did say you have a tendency to daydream at times, but your grades are good so that must not be a problem. She assured us you are most certainly a delightful student."

My mouth flops open. Did she honest-to-goodness say those beautiful words? Does Miss Jennings really like me? I sigh to let out a whole bunch of relief. Some days are better than others. I listen as Auntie Marie says Miss Wolf actually admitted she had made a bad error in judgment, and now I see my aunt through new eyes when I feel she does believe and trust me. Could it be possible that she might even learn to love me? I suppose that's asking for too much.

The past few months have been so hard because Auntie Marie is so strict. I have tried to do what she asks me to do to make her happy. Even though she, Uncle Carl, and Grandma have all been kind and do help me, one important thing is always missing.

I miss Mama so much that it hurts because she is so different from everyone here. Why can't someone in this house hug me once in the while like Mama does? Then I would really and truly feel loved.

Chapter 12

A New Assignment

Jenny

Two months pass and dear Dr. Sutherland has found another opening for me. After I arrive at the home, I unpack my suitcase of the essentials I will require for this position. Most of my clothes are still at Ruth and Cliff's apartment where my family has been kind enough to keep a room open for my belongings and my visits. Now I sleep with Becky because the small bed in her parent's room had to be returned. I am only there one night a week, and Becky is happy with the arrangement as am I.

The room I'm given for this new assignment is austere and nothing like the mansion's fashionable room at my last place of employment. But how thrilled I was when the commitment to that job ended. I had felt uncomfortable since that first night when the terrified Mrs. Granger burst into my room. Although the incident had not repeated itself, I sporadically heard the sound of cries siphoning from the adjoining room.

This mission is not employment for service to a mother who is returning from the hospital and needs help such as that which Dr. Sutherland is in charge of setting up. He did not have an opening similar to that one but learned from a colleague that another family needs assistance and asked if

I'd like the job. In this case, the mother is in a home for the mentally disturbed, and her three young boys need support. My task this time is that of a housekeeper and cook where I'm not employed by the rich but by the financially comfortable. The home is handsome, though seasoned, with four bedrooms plus a room for a domestic, which is now my title.

I put on a blue housedress and tie a white apron around my neck and waist. I was informed my duties will begin immediately, so I proceed to the kitchen where I soon learn the cook who preceded me has not left much in the refrigerator. I give a tiny squeal of delight when I find some leftover roast beef. I bustle through a survey of the baking essentials in the cupboard and find the ingredients for baking powder biscuits. My fingers fly as I peel potatoes that I find in one of the bins. How relieved I am when with a little more probing I uncover enough food to prepare a suitable meal.

"Wow," says Herman who is the oldest boy and about ten years. I watch him spread jam on another of my treats and bite into it. As he chews, he manages to say, "These biscuits are great."

Before long Ronnie, about eight, and Gordon, who is seven, join their brother in praise of my baking. Signs of approval come even from Mr. Schumaker who adds as everyone finishes their tapioca pudding, "A fine meal, Mrs. Westin." *At least a good beginning,* I think to myself. I smile and thank him.

"Would you boys help me clear the table?"

They study me with surprise since I'm sure no one has asked this of them before, but after Herman jumps up to offer his assistance, his brothers follow. Early on I realize that if I am to handle this task, it is best to do it as a team. Surprisingly, it's working.

Not that all days are a success. I work at it and my cinnamon rolls and fancy pies help to bring jubilant grins to the three young faces. Before long their first action when they return from school is poking their noses into the kitchen to see what is for supper. They spread peanut butter and jelly on my homemade bread to make the wait for the evening meal less painful.

I recall my interview with Mr. Schumaker when I convinced him I must have at least one day off a week. That is a necessity as I need rest and an enjoyable visit with my cousin Ruth. He informed me that Friday would be the best day for me to take a day off but would appreciate my waiting until the boys have left for school. My stamp of approval was based on my agreement to return no later than Saturday morning. To date no problem has arisen, and that I appreciate.

Like a flash, I realize I've made a horrible mistake. When I recall it now, I catch my breath and freeze. Good grief, I have completely forgotten to ask for time off at Christmas to keep my promise to Maggie. How stupid of me for it will be most difficult to approach Mr. Schumaker at this late date and I shudder at the very thought. Surely he will know how important this is to me and my family, will he not? I am aware that I must not ask for much time off because if I get greedy, it could force him to refuse my request.

He moves his head up slightly and opens his eyes wide as if to make sure I remember who writes the paychecks. "I'm sorry, Jenny," he informs me, "but the boys will be home for Christmas vacation, and I cannot give you time off then even if it is without pay." A sick smile forms on his face as if he's doing me a favor when he says forcefully and with emphasis, "Don't you understand what the holidays would be like for them without you here? They've come to depend on you and look forward to your guidance and leadership."

My hope falls apart, crashing at my feet. Are the boys more important than my own children? Certainly not to me.

He has never before so much as told me he is satisfied with my work, and this is the closest he's come to making me feel my influence contributed to their nurturing. But not to give me time off to see my own children? I excuse myself and go to my room to shut the door quietly after which I wearily lean against it.

Where these accommodations were acceptable before, now the room looks as sick as I feel. The drab bed, prosaic dresser, bleak chair, and colorless wallpaper all seem to scream at me to remember my place and not make a fuss.

Do not rock the boat, they shout, or you will lose this job that you gravely need.

I stand quietly for a moment before dragging myself like a snail on a cement sidewalk to the tiny desk, pull out a chair and begin writing. "My precious Maggie . . ."

Maggie

Auntie Marie opens Mama's letter, and I am so excited that I almost wet my pants. I am even happier when she hands me a small envelope because this one is special—just for me. I squeeze it in my hand and hurry like crazy to Grandma's room so I can be alone when reading it because I'm sure Mama is telling me what day she will be home for Christmas.

"My precious Maggie," it begins. I can hear Mama say my name right in my head, and I look down to continue reading. "I'm sorry to tell you this and hope you'll understand."

I close my eyes and put the letter in my lap while I sit here hardly breathing because I'm sure I know what comes next. The moment of joy sinks like a roller coaster that abruptly dives downward, surprising my whole body.

Only because I must do this and not because I'm curious do I continue reading. Bad news happens so often now that I wonder why it keeps hurting so much. This time Mama tells me what's stopping her trip. She says, "Honey, I take care of three boys whose mother is very ill and in a sanitarium. That's where they care for sick people for long periods of time. The father of the boys says they'll have no Christmas if I'm not here to make it happy for them."

Now I clench my fists and a quick "I don't care about them" is hurled like a bang out of my mouth. It is maybe the meanest thing I've ever thought or said, but it's for sure I'm not going to apologize to anyone.

I sit quietly for a moment and then continue to read. "Maggie, it breaks my heart to try to make a happy Christmas for them and not my own children. I love you, dear, and hope to make arrangements to see you, David, and Holly soon even if it's not right at Christmas."

I fold the letter neatly and put it on my lap. I rock faster and faster until the rocking makes the letter tumble to the floor. I decide to just leave it there. Three months I've waited and marked days off on the calendar only to now wonder—what for?

Mama doesn't know about me and all the changes I've had to make to get through each day. She doesn't know I'm waiting for her to make me whole, and she doesn't understand that parts of me hurt so much I'm sure I am bruised forever. Waiting seems without end, and I feel my bottom lip quiver and protrude. My eyes prickle with tears that push their way out.

Mostly Mama doesn't understand there is no Christmas without her, Daddy, and my brother and sister. Just no Christmas at all. So there. Our family has broken into tiny pieces and nobody is even trying to put us back together.

I sniff and do not even want to blow my nose. Without any intention on my part, every past Christmas in my life tumbles before me. Multicolored strings of lights swirl around the tree, and then all the house lights are turned off so our family can see every bit of this beauty that includes long tinsel pieces shimmering on every branch. Bright tissue-wrapped packages held together with colorful Christmas seals and ribbons are piled around the tree.

I remember caroling in Laurel Hill with church friends and enjoying the yummy hot cocoa we got after our shivery adventure. I want more than anything to hear my favorite stories about Mama's Christmases when she was a little girl.

Every year she would tell us about how Grandpa would tug at the huge tree that had been cut from a forest near their house and when inside almost touched the ceiling until it was in the center of the living room. She told us that when it was trimmed, Grandpa would light the candles. The family would then join hands and walk very slowly around the tree so they would not bump into the dangerous flame. All this time they would sing Christmas carols, and Mama told us how Grandma's soft, low voice was so beautiful that she and her sisters would want to stop just to listen. When their little brother Lawrence was born and grew big enough, he would join them circling the tree and singing in his clear baby voice.

When we lived in Laurel Hill, the church programs were always a couple days after Christmas and how proud I was to recite the verses I learned. But what I miss most is the laughter and love that went away with Mama.

No, I tell myself I will not cry. I stay seated with arms crossed as I tense my whole body against the pain that crawls up through me like a fountain. I try to convince myself that I am strong enough to stop even a tiny tear from tumbling down my cheek. But like every other time lately, I have no way of stopping it. First one and then one hundred sobs come until a waterfall of tears follows to stop only when it feels like it has filled a lake.

So those boys Mama takes care of will not have a Christmas if she doesn't stay? Don't they have their father? I don't even know where my father is. How about us kids, aren't we important? Guess we're nothing; not to anyone.

My little kitten finds my lap. I know he hates crying and arguments. No matter how loud or soft the noise is, Ted Bear knows if a person is angry or sad, and he does everything he can to stop the suffering. Now he curls up in my lap, trying hard to shoo away my pain. He looks up into my eyes, flattens his long neck upward against my body, and purrs so loud that all I hear is him instead of my heaving sobs.

I try with all my might to stop crying for the sake of my precious kitty who cared enough to find me in this big old house. I'm sure he did that so he could give me love when I needed it most.

I hear Grandma first and then Auntie Marie call me to say food is on the table. I do not go downstairs but do my best to pretend everything is just fine. By now they must know Mama isn't coming for Christmas. Her letter has erased her again just like my name disappeared when I scrubbed it over and over in the school bathroom. But somehow I am still here with all this suffering.

For the first time since I moved into this house, no one comes to make me go downstairs for supper.

Chapter 13

Getting To Know You

Jenny

A recent newspaper reported that the mayor decreed the city and residential districts would not be buying new outdoor Christmas decorations this year because of lack of funds during this economic crisis. As I study the trimmings lining the streets, I feel this is one cutback that will not make folks feel cheated. What was purchased in years past remains spellbinding.

"Did you know, Paul, that I'm in love with the Christmas season and have been since I was a little girl? This is the most exciting time of the year for me, and I couldn't help but pass that on to my children."

He gives me a warm smile. "You enriched their lives with a special gift, Jenny," he says and then focuses on the road ahead.

"I so enjoy it when the street lamps are tastefully decorated and the department store windows display everything from Santa to stunning evening gowns. Oh look, Paul. What a ravishing green dress in that store window, but I am aware that only the rich can afford those frocks."

"Are you envious, Jenny?"

I cannot believe he asked that. "Merciful heavens, no," I tell him before I add, "I'm not jealous in the least." I am also most sincere when I add, "I'd rather be driving through all this beauty than own any of those expensive garments.

Thank you for asking me out tonight or I would have missed this magic. You certainly didn't have to be so kind."

"Remember that I owe you for the pain I caused you at our last meeting. I'm sorry for not realizing how much I was hurting you. Also I did promise you an update on the progress George and I are making for an earlier release of your husband."

As we pull up to the restaurant entrance, the valet hurries to open my door to assist me before my escort reaches my side. Paul gives him the keys to park the car and then takes my arm to escort me to the building where the doorman opens it for us. I haven't dined in any of the more expensive supper clubs in the city, so my anxiety is high as I wait to see this one. For that matter, I do not even have the money to frequent the less expensive downtown cafeterias.

I manage to hold back a gasp so I don't sound like a school girl. How thoughtful that Paul warned me to dress formal as no doubt only the more prominent people patronize this ornate dining establishment. I sense my eyes enlarging with delight as I study the huge room. Tables are overlaid with pink tablecloths and matching napkins, and the wallpaper contains abundant shades of pink nestled into gray and green tones. Oblong mirrors and candles set in sparkling silver holders reflect the candlelight at various points on the walls and give the room its elegant look. In my blue velvet dress with its long sleeves and elegant lace cuffs and trim, I feel as fashionable as other women in the restaurant. How strange that I packed this exquisite dress for Milwaukee. I had no idea I would ever wear it again. Was it a premonition? I know only that when I display it, I feel elegant.

We follow the maître d' across the thick green and gray carpet, and Paul whispers, "I see you wore my favorite dress tonight."

"Your favorite dress?" I'm puzzled. "How could you have seen this before tonight?"

A chair is pulled out for me at a small round table, and I am given a menu. Paul is seated next to me with his eyes twinkling mischievously, but he waits until we are alone.

"I don't mean to embarrass you, Jenny, but do you remember the Ford and Vincent anniversary party in Laurel Hill?"

This leaves me startled. "Come now, don't tell me you were there?"

"Yes, I was but only long enough to have dinner and pay my respects. Unfortunately I had a court case the next morning and had work to finish."

"You didn't embarrass me by saying you've seen this dress before. You of all people know I can't afford new clothes. I'm delighted we share memories of an evening that holds extraordinary recollections for me."

"As it does for me," he adds. The comment confuses me. Why should it hold special remembrances for him? I'm afraid to ask.

"You look lovely once again and are even more striking than when the governor asked you to dance."

"You heard that?" I can hardly believe this.

"I most certainly did. I got up from dinner and strolled toward the head table to thank the Vincents for the evening when I saw the governor approach the table. I held back and heard him say that he would like to dance the next dance with the loveliest woman here tonight."

I feel myself blush and am amazed he remembers the governor's words. To save my embarrassment and curiosity, I begin reading the menu but swallow hard when I note there are no prices listed.

Paul must have caught my expression because he said, "Jenny, don't worry about the cost of the entrees. There's no advantage in taking you to a charming restaurant if you don't select what you truly enjoy. Believe me when I tell you that I'm getting more pleasure out of this than you are."

We make our menu choices, and he orders for both of us. I'm fascinated as I notice our waiter taking no notes.

"I'm not just curious but truly interested in knowing more about you, Jenny. May I ask how you know the Vincents?

Why am I so pleased he's interested? But there's certainly no harm in telling him.

"Paul, I was enchanted with Laurel Hill from the first time I laid eyes on the town. We had little money and were looking forward to Jonathan's employment at the bank. Fortunately we found a lovely upstairs apartment for rent in the Vincent home. Later I discovered Mr. Vincent had been mayor of Laurel Hill several years before we met, and as I got to know him, I learned what a perfect gentleman he is."

"That he is," Paul adds with a smile. "But continue."

"In no time Mrs. Vincent and I became fast friends. We had long chats disclosing our backgrounds, and I received many treasured recipes from her. She told me that William Ford, who I met at the party, and Henry Ford, were related. I must have sat there with my mouth open because I was so impressed. Most people, including me, knew Henry Ford by name only and heard he had developed the assembly line that made the first automobile affordable.

"Even when we got our own home that was one block north of the bank where Jonathan worked, we kept in close touch with the Vincents. Mrs. Vincent told me that since the William Fords and she and her husband were married on the same date, they'd decided to celebrate the occasion together. The Vincents insisted we sit beside them at the head table.

"I was truly honored. I knew Governor Green had been invited by the Fords. Paul, you know the rest of the story about that great evening that I'll never forget."

Paul was watching me with an interested expression and semi-smile on his face during all the time I was telling the background of the occasion. I know the story was interesting, but he didn't seem to miss a thing. Was he this way with his clients? I'm sure I would have made a comment had not the server been on his way to our table with our soup.

The evening progresses in a much different manner than our first dinner together. We discuss trivial things and realize we have many common interests. We talk politics but do not argue; instead we respect each other's opinion. I hear new slants on civic problems and feel he listens and considers many of my beliefs.

I find Paul fascinating and sense my face becoming flushed. There must be a glow about me because when the waiter returns to set our salad and rolls before us, he asks, "You two appear so happy. Are you celebrating a special anniversary?" At first his remark puzzles me until I lower my eyes and see my wedding ring sparkling on my finger. Then it is clear that he believes we are married and this might be an anniversary.

Paul does not let a moment pass before saying, “Yes, a very special one.”

After the waiter leaves, I am sure my facial expression wears a teasing twinkle when I ask Paul, “And just what anniversary is that?”

Much to my disappointment, he quickly changes the subject and tells me he has met with George and knows they are making progress. At this stage, he says there is little to report but gives me encouragement when he confesses he is elated with even a small glimpse of hope.

I am so engrossed in our conversation that I do not notice when a few musicians file onto the stage carrying instruments. Then alluring sounds fill the room and Paul asks if I would like to dance. I assure him I would, and we weave between tables and glide across the expanse of the dance floor. A soloist carols the words of a melody that is unfamiliar, so I pay close attention to retain the words as long as possible. The lyric is electrifying and touches my heart in an unexpected way.

“So kiss me, my sweet,
And so let us part;
And when I grow too old to dream,
That kiss will live in my heart.”

I’m only too aware that something strange is happening to me. I’m perplexed as I recall that Jonathan was not a ballroom dancer and refused to take me to dances unless they were of some importance. I deeply missed the many joys of dancing because I know I’m quite good at it. What I am thinking might sound juvenile, but to me, the rhythm of the music lifts me to new heights. I must admit Jon was within his rights when he countered my wistful desires with, “Why should I take you hopping around the room when I do not even know how to dance with any grace? Do you go to ball games with me?” Sadly that is true, but this is yet further evidence of how little we have in common.

Now as Paul holds me in his arms and slowly guides me gracefully around the dance floor, something long lost stirs within me. But guilt quickly consumes me as I remember this man is Jon's lawyer, and I must not read something into this that does not exist just because I am an incurable romantic. He only asked me here tonight as a kind gesture and because the evening had been agonizing for me the last time we were together when he told me the length of time before Jonathan's release. When we return to the table, I am still shaken but cautious. I'm also a bit distant in my attempt to hide my troubled emotions. Perhaps it would be helpful if I were to confide to Paul my recent disappointment being unable to get time off at Christmas? It's definitely worth a try.

"Maybe you can help me with something that is bothering me?"

"Anything," he says.

To give me time to determine the most effective way to handle this, I butter a roll I have no intention of eating and put it on my small plate.

"This is a bit difficult because I must admit my stupidity." I pause; he says nothing. "When I interviewed for my present job, I failed to ask for a few days off during the Christmas holidays. Worst of all, some time ago I promised my oldest daughter Maggie that I would be home for Christmas."

Paul doesn't appear to be upset. "Your employer did give you time off, didn't he?"

"No."

His expression changes immediately. "Jenny, this could be a terrible blow to your daughter."

Terrible is hardly the word, I tell myself. The blow has no doubt already happened since she must have received my letter by now.

"I've written her already, Paul, telling her Mr. Schumaker informed me the boys would be home for the holidays with no one to care for them and informed me he definitely could not spare me at this time. Oh, Paul, I'm sure I included that in Maggie's letter."

Silence follows that is torture to me.

"Is this Schumaker a widower or divorce'?" Paul asks.

I shove my plate aside. "Neither, Paul. His wife is in an institution for the mentally ill, and I haven't met her as yet."

"Does this man have parents who could help? For that matter, in-laws?"

Then I remember.

"At one time I heard him mention that when his wife is home, her mother comes from Chicago to help with her daughter's care."

"That's it then," he says with a grin that looks like he has discovered gold. "I dislike being judge and jury in this case, but wouldn't he want his wife home over the Christmas holiday? Couldn't her mother visit a little early and care for the boys? She might enjoy that since she is their grandmother."

My goodness, why didn't I think of that? Paul certainly knows how to come up with the answers; no wonder he is a lawyer.

Out of the corner of my eye, I see the waiter returning with our tempting prime ribs. Can they be as good as they look? When he leaves, I sample the feast and wonder if I have ever tasted anything more satisfying. The meat is tender and full-flavored, the baked potato is fluffy and topped with melted butter, and the vegetables are colorful and well-done just to my liking.

When we finish dinner, I lose no time returning to our current subject.

"You most certainly have given me something to think about, Paul. I now understand how selfish my employer is, and if he must get along without me I'm convinced he can do it." But something else becomes clear, and my voice drops.

"Paul, this is but a dream. I can't very well announce to that arrogant individual that I'm going to spend Christmas in Duluth and demand that he make other arrangements."

"And why not?"

"Because I might lose my job, that's why."

"Jenny, I'm so convinced that will never happen that I'm willing to make a bet. If you lose your job, I'll pay your lost wages until you find employment."

I look at him as if he's donned a Santa suit. "Paul, don't tease. I saw that twinkle in your eye. You're enjoying this, aren't you, and do believe Mr. Schumaker will fire me if I insist on going home for a few days."

"I most certainly do not."

After a pause I tell him, "All right, Mr. Foolhardy, you've got yourself a bet. But if you lose, I warn you that you deserve it for taking such a foolish risk."

My words shock even me. Actually, I'm frightened. Is he serious? Will I have the courage to go through with this?

"I'm certain it's already too late," I say. "Maggie believes I won't be home for Christmas. Dare I change those plans at this late date?"

"Does Maggie like surprises?"

"That's a silly question. Don't all children? Of course, she does."

"Then present her with her biggest surprise ever," he suggests. "She'll never forget it, and what a great Christmas that will be for both of you. Jenny, I'm serious. If you lose your job, let my money be a gift to you and your children."

I knew that would be the greatest gift anyone could ever give me. But am I really considering taking money from this man who is to me barely beyond the category of a stranger?

"Let me think about it," I tell him for lack of anything else to say.

"Does that mean you'll let me see you after Christmas to confirm who wins? The first time I'm in town?"

"I suppose the answer must be *yes* because if this goes wrong, I'll need money even if it's a loan."

"No loan," Paul says with a firmer voice than I ever imagined he possessed. "Let's shake on it."

Our conversation reverts to lighter subjects, and we dance once more before I tell him I have to leave early in the morning for work. As much as I hate to leave, I must get back to Ruth's apartment soon if I'm to have any pep for tomorrow's work.

We walk to the car perhaps not even aware we have joined hands and are laughing about something we both find whimsical. It doesn't take long to reach what I now call home. As the car pulls up in front, Paul brings up the Christmas subject again.

"Don't disappoint your children, Jenny. If things go wrong when you inform Mr. Schumaker, you absolutely must spend Christmas with your children. If this bothers you, remember this. I can easily afford to lose this bet. I have no family except my mother and sister, and they're both self-sufficient." As he speaks, he grasps my hand and squeezes it firmly. "Thank you, my dear, for this evening. I totally enjoyed your company."

"I'm the one to be grateful," I say. "It even topped that anniversary party in Laurel Hill. After all, you're a better dancer than the governor."

We laugh as Paul walks me to the door of the building. When we stop, I am aware he is studying me.

"By the way, Paul, you answered the waiter's question by saying we were celebrating a special anniversary. Just what anniversary is that?"

"I thought you knew. The anniversary of our first date." Again he clasps my hand, but this time brings it to his lips and kisses it before turning around and walking briskly to his car.

Chapter 14

What's Wrong With Me?

Maggie

Even though I'm wearing a long nightgown, thick socks, and a heavy robe, I'm so cold that I shiver as I stand by Grandma's bedroom window. Every day Uncle Carl says he gets up early to shovel coal into the furnace. Somehow today it takes longer for the warm air to find its way upstairs where we are, but that doesn't really matter. I don't care if I'm warm or cold because what difference does it make? Nothing matters anymore.

A light snowfall dusts the ground like when Grandma sifts powdered sugar over her special chocolate cake. The sky has been dark all week, but as I stand by the window to watch as the wind gets stronger, I feel as though I am hidden behind a sudden shower of snow flurries. I don't want to get going with this day but stand hypnotized, staring as a heap of snow tumbles from the corner of our roof and plops into an already huge pile of dirty snow. It reminds me of all the strange things that have been happening to me this past year when first something happy happens to bring me great joy and then later crumples like breaking glass when it turns to sadness and breaks my heart.

Is something wrong with me? If that's true, how can I even describe my problem? I see pretty things and yet everything feels like it can't move. Why am I not able to figure out what's happening to me?

Before Mama's letter came, I was so excited I could barely wait for Christmas because she promised to visit. When the snow began to fall this Saturday morning, my first thought should have been to grab Tommy and dash with him outside to make snow angels. Normally I would have begged to take my little cousin sliding down the hill on the sled his daddy made for him. So why didn't I do that? Without Mama's visit, I feel like I'm some kind of statue waiting to come to life.

Can even adults help me? Maybe not because I have never heard anyone talk about feeling this way. Is my whole body slowly dying? I only know one thing, and that is it began with Mama's letter and now won't go away. I sit in Grandma's rocker and move back and forth, again and again.

Before long they'll surely call me for breakfast, which is pure torture because I'm sure I can't eat. It hurts so much to do that little bitty thing that I might just scream as I never get hungry anymore. Everyone at the table stares at me like they're counting the minutes until I open my mouth and chew since they're so sure it will make me feel better. They just don't catch on at all. The only thing trying to eat does is make me nervous, and I get so tired working at being cheerful that sometimes I can't even talk. My gosh, I don't even argue with Auntie Marie anymore.

As I continue to watch out the window, my mind speeds up as if having a race with the blowing wind. Our class had many Christmas activities, but even those weren't fun for me this year. In our projects class, I made a green and white button box for Mama and then knew there was even trouble with that like how am I supposed to give it to her when she's so far away? And everyone was excited about the school program except me. For a while, I tried to do my part but felt like a puppet waiting for someone to push me along. "Doggone it," I now say loud and clear. Nothing at all seems right.

I yank on a heavy blue flannel blouse and a gray pleated skirt before fastening long woolen socks to garters. I choose a heavy sweater because the more clothes I wear, the safer I feel. Goodness gracious but my skirt is getting loose.

"Mag . . . gee." That's Aunt Marie's angry voice coming from far away. "Your food is getting cold." Goose bumps pop up on my arms not because I'm cold but because I'm being pulled downstairs by her command.

As usual I say little as I pick at my hard-boiled egg and tear my toast into tiny bits. I still feel funny when without even looking up I feel popping eyes watching my every move. As if this isn't bad enough, Auntie Marie says, "I'd like to see you in my room when you finish your breakfast, Maggie."

Just what I need—a talk with Auntie Marie.

Ten minutes later, I shuffle into her bedroom. I know I should pick up my feet, but what's the use? Auntie Marie is seated on the bench of her dressing table and motions for me to sit in Tommy's wooden rocker—not that it fits me but I manage because it has no side supports.

I cross my arms and rest them on my stomach before bending over a little to stare at the floor. I don't feel like looking into anyone's eyes, especially Auntie Marie's. I can feel her studying me, and she must think I'm weird and probably wonders what she should say next. Is this the test I need so that maybe grown-ups can help me?

"I've tried to be patient with you," Aunt Marie begins speaking slower than usual. "I've about run out of ideas. I know you're disappointed and hurt that your mother can't keep her promise to come home for Christmas. I know she will try to get here soon. Can't you be thankful and at least look forward to that?"

The only sound in the room is the swaying back and forth of the small rocker. I could tell her about my problem, but what would she think? I'm not sure Auntie will even know what I'm talking about though I promise myself to try before making up my mind. It's so hard to say the words, but I breathe deeply and talk as fast as I can so I won't change my mind.

"I'm scared, Auntie Marie."

"Scared? Of what?"

"Something is wrong inside me 'cause I feel unhappy all the time. Oh, Auntie Marie, please help me because I don't know what's going on with this brand new feeling. I'm sick with sadness and don't know why. What I really need is to talk to Mama about this because I miss my whole family more than I can say especially now when I remember how much we enjoyed Christmas together. If she at least could have come, I would have had her with me."

There, I've done it. Even if Auntie doesn't know how to help me, I feel a speck better because I've told someone.

Auntie Marie shifts on the bench. Everything grows quiet again as she waits like she's trying to find the right words. I understand how that feels.

"Oh, honey, I know," Auntie finally says. "But your family isn't here, and we're doing all we can to be your family. Don't you understand that? Maybe it will help if I tell you about other people's pain."

Other people hurt? I think about what she just said, but I'm sure other people don't have a huge lump inside them like I have. The pain fills me up so there's no room for anything else.

But now I forget my own thoughts and listen as Auntie Marie continues because she sounds like she is filled with understanding and pity and not bossiness like she usually is. "There's sadness not only for you, Maggie, because so many have lost jobs and folks have no money. Sadly they're without homes and food, and families are torn apart, not just yours. Some folks even have to put their children temporarily in orphanages when the adults must be sent to poor farms."

I frown and stare into my aunt's eyes to make sure she isn't just making this up. As I look at the sadness on her face, I believe it must be true. Now when Auntie Marie continues, I pay attention.

"At night men who have no home or jobs huddle on the street corners around burning trash cans to keep warm and stay alive. They survive on one meal a day that is sometimes only soup from church kitchens. When the stock market crashed, many men jumped out of windows or killed themselves in some other way. I'm not sure, but they probably believed they could no longer exist if they weren't rich and couldn't provide for their families. That was a poor choice as so many children were then without fathers, which is worse than being without money. The whole world is upside down because of these hard times."

I sit quietly and want to cry. I knew we had very little money, but I thought that was only in our house. So why hasn't anyone told me about these hard times for everybody; not even in school have I heard these stories.

If Aunt Marie wasn't telling me this to make me feel better, then I am sure I'm not the only one going through this sadness. I begin to wonder about something else. Wouldn't it be better if our family lived together happily rather than living apart and hurting like this? Right now we're all suffering alone because we're not together like a family should be.

I turn again to Auntie Marie. "Why aren't we talking about this in school?

"Perhaps because each child is different, and parents must determine the time it is best for their children to begin discussions about the hard times we're going through. Most parents want their child to be spared this unrest and sadness until they are old enough to accept the pain of a Great Depression. The responsibility is not that of the school but belongs to the parents.

"Maggie, you know that you're affecting everyone in this household, don't you?" My mouth pops open in surprise as I gawk at her while trying to understand this new trouble. What she just said makes no sense because why should it bother other people if I feel bad? That's dumb.

"You apparently aren't mindful, Maggie, that moods are contagious," Marie says. "When we see happy people, our spirits lift, and before long we're laughing with them."

Well, by golly, now Auntie Marie makes sense. I tell her, "I didn't mean to make anyone else miserable and didn't even know I was doing that. It's just that since Mama's letter came I've been so upset. Believe me, I didn't do this on purpose."

"I appreciate that," says Aunt Marie, and her voice sounds kind. As I watch her, I gulp because she bends down to get on her knees to hug me; well, just a little, before giving me a kiss on my cheek. She hasn't done that in all the time I've lived here.

"I know, dear, that I'm very strict and have set up many rules. Do you know why?" She lets go of me to look me right in my eyes. “It’s because when you first came here, you weren’t used to direction. You were getting away with things a child should not do. Now don’t misunderstand me when I say this because I love your mother even though we have different ways of raising children. I couldn’t take on the responsibility of having you here if you were a problem to our family.”

For a moment I feel like I can see things out of my aunt’s eyes. I’m beginning to get this new idea; well, at least a little bit. I’d better not be any trouble or they might put me in an orphanage. Or even sell me to the gypsies like people sometimes do. Oh my goodness, would they do that to me?

“Have I been doing okay, Auntie Marie?” I sit waiting for an answer not knowing what more to say.

She rises and sits on the bench again. A smile crosses her face. “Actually, dear, you’ve been better than I dared hope at least until you learned your mother wouldn’t be here for Christmas. After talking with you now, I must admit I grasp the way you are thinking far better than I did before.”

I feel like I’ve been tucked in a warm blanket.

“I know this isn’t a happy Christmas for you,” Aunt Marie says, “but remember all the people who won’t have Christmas at all. Don’t be surprised, dear, if I ask for a present from you. It won’t cost money but will take effort on your part.”

Puzzled, I answer. “What do you mean, Auntie Marie?”

She speaks slowly; maybe so there will be no misunderstanding. “Try as hard as you can to appear happy,” she says. “Smile often because it’s magic and will keep you from being sad. Who knows, that might even help you to hurt less. Do you think you can do that?”

I answer hesitantly. “Well, I can try. If you really think it will make everyone happier then I’ll work at it really hard.”

Auntie Marie rises but continues talking. *Just like my aunt, I think to myself.* So she won’t waste time, she gets ready for the next thing she must do while still doing the first thing. I’ve seen it happen lots of times before. I follow her out of the room wondering how to begin all these changes. Then she surprises me by slowing down and turning to face me as if she’s just thought of something else.

"Maggie it's about time I share a powerful Norwegian secret with you." She bends down to look me straight in the eyes. "When you're sad or upset, *work.*"

The word *work* comes out really loud. "That means," she continues, "do the hardest and busiest physical work you can do. Soon it will take over your thinking and change the way you feel."

I try as hard as I can not to giggle. I would never have thought of work. I was thinking "magic wand" kinds of things, but Auntie Marie was thinking brooms. When I study the serious expression on her face, I don't dare tell her that by mistake she almost cheered me up.

As the day continues, I find changing my mood was easier than I thought it would be. First I make a really hard effort to be thankful for what I have got right now. Then I know I must try much harder not to dwell on what I do not have. I say a prayer for all the poor people in the world especially those who haven't a warm home or food to eat and those who must live in orphanages. I even decide to take Auntie Marie seriously about the Norwegian secret. But I certainly hope other Norwegian secrets are more interesting.

In Laurel Hill, it was the family's custom to wear Sunday-best clothes on Christmas Eve to make us look special when celebrating the birth of Jesus. That would be silly here. My goodness, I'm sure Grandma doesn't have any special clothes like that and Uncle Carl, Auntie Marie, and Tommy? Well, maybe.

But something special *is* happening. Grandma said we're going to sit at the dining room table tonight and use the good china she packed in her trunk while in Norway and brought all the way across the ocean. I handle every piece carefully as I take it from her built-in china closet because I know it means so much to my dear grandma that it means lots to me. Helping her set the table for dinner tonight makes me feel trusted and grown up. Now I'm really trying.

Something weird is coming over me. I begin to feel a little hungry. At this moment, it's a strange feeling because I haven't felt like this in weeks.

Someone opens and shuts the back door. I hurry to see who it is, but it's only our next-door neighbor, Mrs. Helstrom. She never waits for permission to come in but enters as if the kitchen is somehow connected to her house. Of course, she has a telephone when we can't afford one, so maybe she has a message for someone. She stands talking to Uncle Carl, but since I cannot hear what they're saying, I go back to the dining room to continue my task.

I like the jolly lady who is so bouncy that her whole body tells stories all by itself even if she doesn't say a word. Her stomach shakes as she roars with laughter.

When Grandma returns to the dining room, she tells me Uncle Carl has to do an urgent errand for our neighbor and pick up something downtown. It must be important to go way down there, but then it's Christmas so Uncle Carl would never turn her down tonight.

"It's a good thing he got a secondhand car last week, isn't it, Grandma?"

Earlier I had heard Auntie Marie say it might have been a bad idea to buy the car since Uncle Carl will be laid off in January during the slow season at the icebox plant where he works. Sometimes the layoff lasts two months. But I heard Auntie also say that this year they might have to shut down the plant for good, and that makes everyone very nervous. Since they had already saved most of the money to buy the car and Auntie Marie is working steady, she told Uncle Carl to buy it anyway. Having the car is good, but tonight it's causing a delay in serving dinner when I'm really hungry. The greatest torment is the smell of the stuffed turkey roasting in the oven.

I need to find some things in the pantry to put on the table, so I go back to the kitchen where Tommy sits coloring in a book while the ladies attend to the cooking. Little Ted Bear has glued himself directly in front of the stove, and he just won't budge. I watch him raise his little head and sniff the air. Grandma bends down to pet him and says to be patient as he'll get plenty of turkey scraps. Now that's a lot for Grandma to say to a cat.

Ted Bear has charmed everyone, even Auntie Marie. I fetch the salt and pepper when I hear the front door open. Thank goodness, Uncle Carl must be back.

"Merry Christmas," a cheerful voice calls in greeting.

I stop. That's a woman's voice and not Uncle Carl's. Is it Mrs. Helstrom? No, but then I hear that voice again in my head. Could it be?

I trip over my feet and in a split-second dash like a shooting star to the front door with everyone following me. There stands my precious, dear Mama. I'm so surprised that it's impossible to find words, and I can hardly breathe.

Tiny lace and tinsel-like snow is scattered in Mama's rich auburn hair. To me, she resembles a fairy princess, and her coat is her royal robe. When she reaches for me, I throw myself into her waiting arms and am filled with instant joy.

I hug her with all my stored love. She then strokes my head, and for the first time in all these months, there are happy tears in my eyes instead of the sad ones.

Chapter 15

Do I Still Have A Job?

Jenny

It's a challenge to keep up with Ruth's flying fingers, but I do my part to dry the dishes as quickly as I can. Cliff met me at the bus depot late this afternoon, and we headed for the apartment and the evening meal Ruth had prepared after which he was off to a lodge meeting. That suits us fine since we want desperately to visit, but before that can be fulfilled, there's another interruption from the other room.

"Mama, I'm thirsty. Can Aunt Yenny bring me some water?" Ruth chuckles and smiles at me. "You'd better do it, Jenny, or she'll never settle down because she gets so wound up when you're here."

By the time I fill the request and tell another expeditious fable to the curly-headed tot, Ruth has finished the evening tasks.

"She's tickled pink to have you back, Jenny. You've made quite a friend."

"Becky's friendship is not a one-way street, Ruth. I adore the little pumpkin."

We both pull up a chair to enjoy the dessert we've saved until now. As I add the cream and sugar to my coffee, I recall a comment Mother used to make about Scandinavians. "If you add enough cream and sugar to your coffee, it makes no difference if it's fresh or reheated," she'd say.

"A wealth of knowledge from Nelly," Ruth grins as she clinks her cup to mine. "So your visit went okay with Holly and David as well?"

I go into detail about the enjoyment I had on Christmas Day when Alma and Jake invited Maggie and me to their home for dinner. Alma is an exceptional cook, which is apparent from the size of both their bodies.

"It was like a gift from heaven to see my children together again. Maggie hasn't been with her siblings in months even though Holly and David have the benefit of seeing each other frequently. It's most understandable since those responsible for the care of the younger ones are Jonathan's mother and sister. What concerns me is no one seems to understand that it's important to at least sporadically get all three siblings together.

"Maggie clung to me, Ruth, as if I'd disappear if I were out of her sight. I encouraged her to set her dreams on the upcoming summer when Grandma and Marie's family would spend time at the lake cottage. That child has a compelling need to have something to look forward to.

"It certainly was a benevolent move on Paul's part to encourage you to spend Christmas with your family."

I reach out for her hand as I softly tell her what is so close to my heart. "Ruth, I can't ever remember having a friend who is so understanding. I'm more grateful to that man than I can express in words."

"Do you expect you'll have much trouble when you go to your job tomorrow?"

"I have no idea," I tell her as I shudder at the thought of facing my employer. Although I can read most people, Mr. Schumaker is a very strange man, and I have no idea what he might say."

When I return to work the next morning, I expected my employer to be angry and possibly terminate me for standing firm on spending the holiday in Duluth with my children. To my complete surprise, Mr. Schumaker is most gracious. He tells me he took time off from work to be with his family and assures me it all worked out. The whole episode puzzles me, and I continue thinking about it while unpacking my belongings to prepare for the day's work.

But nothing equips me for meeting his wife when she's wheeled in to lunch. Pearl Schumaker is bent forward in her chair with her head hanging to one side, and she's obviously unable to lift it. She appears melancholy with her eyes glued to the floor. She says nothing, and it's impossible to understand if she can comprehend the conversation or anything that's going on.

Earlier her husband informed me that his wife would return to the sanitarium tomorrow, but her mother would be with the family for a few additional days before she must return to Chicago. The elderly woman has a need to spend welcome hours with her daughter at the institution and also anticipates the joy of spending additional hours with her grandsons before their Christmas holiday ends.

Her mother sits beside Pearl to feed her the chicken sandwich and jello salad I prepared. An occasional sentence or two is heard from the boys, but other than that, the food is devoured in an unusually quiet manner. A murmur of appreciation circles the table as I serve my freshly baked bread pudding to each diner before I pass the cream and sugar. Then the room falls silent again, and though I've been instructed to take meals with the family, I now hunger for my tasks to be only cooking and providing service. Tonight it's a delight for me to excuse myself to proceed with the cleanup. I tell the boys there is no need for them to help me tonight, and they actually appear to be disappointed.

While the deranged woman naps, her likeable mother joins the boys in the living room to assemble a puzzle. For anyone watching this, the sight takes on the illusion of a contented family spending time together in the beauty of decorations that include an evergreen tree sparkling with lights and tinsel.

The day's duties completed, I excuse myself and go to my room. I have a slight headache and want nothing but to retire early. I know now that I would never make an acceptable nurse in this field as I haven't been exposed to the mentally ill until now. It would take some time for me to adjust to someone like Mrs. Schumaker.

The room is bathed in the inky blackness of night when I awake from a shallow sleep. I sense another presence in the room not far from me that terrifies me, and I reach out only to have my fingers touch the burly mustache of a man. By now, I'm fully awake and open my mouth to scream, but before any sound emerges, his hand slams over my lips and I hear his anxious voice plead, "Don't, please don't. I just want to talk to you."

I recognize the voice of my employer. What is he doing in my bedroom at this hour?

He lifts his hand as I say, "Perhaps you want to talk to me but I don't want to talk to you. You can discuss whatever is bothering you tomorrow morning."

"No," he insists, "I want to talk to you now. Can't I stay with you tonight?"

He wants to stay with me tonight, he says, as if I don't know what's on his mind? The very thought of him even kissing me makes me swallow hard against the nausea rising in my throat. "I want you out of this room *now*," I tell him, speaking almost too loud. "I don't even want you here for another moment." I am aware by this time that my weapon is Pearl's mother being in the house, and he most certainly wouldn't want her to know what he's proposed.

"If you don't go now," I threaten, "I'll count to three and then if you're not gone, I'll scream for help."

I hear the sound of a chair moving, a door opening and closing, and know I've won this battle. Would there be another encounter after his mother-in-law leaves? But of course. My time here is about over; I'll see to that. I have no desire to face either his anger or his lust. Without a doubt, he will be very rude to me now that I have slammed the door on his advances.

Chapter 16

Lake Diamond

Maggie

On our way out of Duluth, we're climbing the steep hill on the way to the cabin, and Uncle Carl's car sounds like it's moaning. I know it's a good car because when we get to the top of the hill, it peps up like Popeye has fed it spinach.

We've been driving for a long time, but it takes forever to get to the Bailey turnoff. I'm getting anxious so ask Auntie Marie how much time it takes from Duluth to get to that town, and she tells me an hour. I don't have a watch, but what I do know is that Uncle Carl drives so slow I can almost count the pieces of grass growing along the highway.

Maybe if I sit back and rest, the time will go faster. At least, this car is much better than the one Grandma's cousin owns that we rode in last winter. That old car had no windows; only heavy side curtains that hung in the window openings to flap and bang as we drove. I was darned scared because cold air was everywhere and turned us into chunks of ice. Well, almost.

Uncle Carl's car is swell. I've studied it, and it's built with straight lines something like a railroad box car that the big bosses ship what they make in. Uncle Carl also has something above his front outside window that he calls a steel visor. He makes it bend down when it's sunny to keep the sun from shining into his eyes. It's neat. There are running boards on both sides, and he showed me the spare tire attached to the back of the car for when we get a flat tire. Best of all, the glass windows crank up and down. I don't ever want to ride in a car without windows again.

When we reach Bailey, we turn onto a bumpy dirt road. The floor boards shake like crazy when the tires drive on the gravel, and I get scared the car will rip apart. But it doesn't, and we drive a little ways until finally the road gets smoother. Yeah! Up and down we go on these funny roads until Uncle Carl speeds up a hill and sails over the top before he puts his foot on the brake. "Whee," Tommy and I squeal because our tummies tickle. We giggle like crazy kids and beg for more.

Before long, we pass a tiny white church, lots of farmhouses, and then the road turns off to the right. We go by one more farmhouse and then start down a steep hill. I don't hear the tires on the dirt road anymore, so I peek out the window and see grass growing right up to the running board. For goodness sake, what kind of a road is this? Half way down, Uncle Carl stops the car to get out and open a wooden gate with a barbed wire fence next to it.

"Uncle Carl, why is that fence here?"

He grins at me. "That, Maggie, is to keep the cows from escaping the Thorngren property." He points to the back of their farmhouse. "Do you see that pump behind the Thorngren house? That's where we've been given permission to fill our pails with drinking water to carry back to the cabin."

"We have to do that? Doesn't the cabin have faucets like in town?" Before he answers and while we continue downhill, I see a lake and a small white building.

"There it is," Auntie Marie announces as if it's the king's palace. I squint and study it but say nothing. That little building—can it really be the lake cottage? I thought it would be a great, big house like grandma's that's in town.

When we stop and park close to the cabin, Tommy wiggles out of the car. He looks so much better since Uncle Carl convinced Aunt Marie to cut his curly locks. Now he has thick, blond waves and knows that people won't mistake him for a girl.

Auntie Marie motions for me to carry the wicker basket. I do as she says, but it's heavy and bangs against my leg. "Ouch" slips out before I can stop it. She asks if the basket is too difficult for me to carry, but I'm going to prove to her that I can do it even if it kills me. That's what my Mama always says.

Auntie's footsteps are close behind me, and I walk as fast as I can on the narrow path so she won't get there before me. At times, I waddle but keep my balance. It's so darned hard to hurry because I'm watching the trees near the pines, and they look like something I've seen before. I wish I could walk slower to study them.

A tiny building on the right grabs my attention. I point to it with my free hand as I see it has a small window on one side and a tall door fastened with a padlock—plus a slanted roof.

"Auntie, what's that?"

"The outhouse," she says. Outhouse? My goodness, what a funny name.

I'm still puzzled, and this strange feeling continues to bother me. Then I remember. When we lived in Laurel Hill, we had many fun times on the lakeshores of Lake Superior near town. After Daddy parked the car, we walked through tree-shaded areas like this that ended up on the sandy beaches where we'd sun, wade, and enjoy our picnic lunches. It feels like Laurel Hill here, and now I'm really excited.

A voice blasts through the air, and I jump. "Stop where you are, young man," Auntie Marie yells at Tommy before she turns to me. "Maggie, catch Tommy and keep an eye on him so he doesn't tumble down the hill or get too near the water." I drop my basket and take off like a bullet exploding from a gun because although I've been instructed to mind her, I'm anxious to see the beach and Grandpa's dock that I've heard so much about.

The cabin is on high ground, and the path to the lake is narrow and steep. Tommy grasps my hand, and his anxiety yanks me along the bumpy trail.

"Hey, Tommy, slow down," I say in a bossy way. I notice he's clinging to a small pail and scoop. That's good because he's got something to keep him busy so he won't bother me.

I get my little cousin settled and look around. This beach that's bordered by huge rocks isn't very big. The beaches by Laurel Hill stretched as far as my eyes could see, and the sand was white and dry. Nothing here looks or feels like that. This sand is dark and damp, but at least, there's enough to keep a little boy amused for a while.

I know the dock is Grandpa's pride and joy because I've heard it's built like docks in Norway. Uncle Carl said the kind farmers around here directed their horses to move those boulders and pile them close together in the lake before he and Grandpa could put wooden boards on top of all of them. Grandpa's huge dock extends a long way from the shore. Uncle Carl and Grandpa did all that work and built the cabin last summer.

Do you suppose the dock will hold me if I walk on it? Hey, these wooden boards are heavier than I thought. When I get to the end, I find many poles sticking up in the air. What do you suppose they're for? Can they be to tie our boat to them? Oh my goodness, do we have a boat? I look around but don't see one. There's so much here that I don't understand.

I wind my arms around one of the poles. The platform I'm standing on has thicker boards than I had at the beginning of the dock. It's the warmest day of the year so far, and as I look up at the blue sky with its white fluffy clouds, the bright sun escapes from one of them, and I squint to shut out the blinding glare. Aunt Marie says it gets warmer when we get farther away from Duluth with its chilling breezes. Tommy seems to be having fun scooping sand into his pail while the sun makes his blond hair sparkle.

This is different from being in town. The only thing that makes noise here is the quiet washing of waves along the shore. This lake and cabin are better than I ever imagined they might be, and I can almost feel the knots untie in my insides.

Some kids are laughing in the distance, so I turn to look across the vacant lot. Three girls are skipping down a road that has lots of pine trees on the lake side. Two of the girls are tall and look strong as if they have heaps of muscles, but the third is small and thin. She's probably younger and more like me. They all wear patterned dresses that hang loosely to just below their knees, and they cross the vacant lot next door to reach us but stop first to say something to Tommy.

"You've grown and don't have curls anymore," one of the older girls says as she fluffs the little boy's blond waves. He beams as he looks up at her. Oh, golly, now I remember! Tommy was here last summer, and they must have gotten acquainted then.

The younger girl calls *Hi* to me. She has cropped brown hair and a face covered with freckles. The pattern of her dress is faded, and her tennis shoes look like they're worn. But when she smiles, she looks very pretty.

"What's your name?" she asks as she comes near me.

"Maggie. Maggie Westin. I'm Tommy's cousin."

"Glad to meet 'cha, Maggie," the girl says warmly as she points in the direction of the road the girls came down. "We live at the top of the hill, and these are my twin sisters, Doris and Elizabeth who we call Liz for short." They nod and wave hi, but they don't look like twins. The only thing that's alike about them is their short brown hair. Doris is quiet while Liz overflows with pep. I nod my head. Shyly I ask the younger girl her name.

"It's Joanna. Joanna Kelly."

"Hi, Joanna."

"Tommy is so adorable." she says. He's filling his pail with wet sand, and now the twins are down on their knees with him as they tip his pail upside down. "Oh, look, Maggie. They're teaching him to make sand castles. He'll love that."

Joanna steps up on the dock with confidence and waddles toward me spreading her arms like a huge bird. I suppose that's so she doesn't fall on the narrow boards. When I came out to the end of the dock, I walked carefully and took my time, but Joanna looks like she's been doing this all her life.

"How old are you?" she asks.

"I'm eight."

"Me too." Joanna says with a smile.

"What grade?"

"I'm finishing the third."

"Know what, Joanna, that's same as me." I like this girl and would like her for my friend. I move back to the edge of the board to make room for her to sit next to me.

"You gonna spend the summer here when school is out?" Joanna asks.

"Probably only weekends because my aunt and uncle both have jobs and work in Duluth."

Joanna frowns, gets on her stomach to lean over the edge of the dock, and then runs her hand through the water. "Oh, I was hoping we could swim together after I do chores."

"But I don't even know how to swim."

Joanna straightens, leans on her elbow, and looks at me. She tells me I don't have to worry about that because her sisters are great swimmers and can teach me. "I can help too," she says. Just then I get a grand idea. "Maybe Grandma Nelly can stay here with Tommy and me when Aunt Marie and Uncle Carl are in Duluth so we don't have to go back and forth." After I say that, I wonder if I even dare hope for such a wonderful wish.

When the girls leave and Tommy is alone, he tells me he's tired of playing in the sand. "I'll beat 'cha," he says as he gets up and runs with me after him. We struggle up the steep path, and I stop to look at the roots of the pine tree on my left. They're like huge steps to help us as we climb the hill. I glance upward through a bunch of branches and can barely see the top of this tree. The trunk looks big and fat like a lady who is going to have a baby.

Tommy and I go through the narrow porch with benches on the side to enter the large room that faces the lake. This is much bigger than I guessed it would be. Uncle Carl has removed all the boards that he covered the windows with last fall, and now sunlight floods the room. The two windows that face the lake are wide and look heavy, and Uncle Carl grasps the bottom of one to swing it up and fasten it to two hooks on the ceiling. Now that the window is out of the way, the fresh lake air steams into the room. It smells wonderful.

I study the window before I tell him, "That window looks like a door that's turned sideways."

"Maggie," he says with surprise. "You hit the nail right on the head. Last summer when Grandpa and I added to this room, we thought a window like this might allow more fresh air to enter the room and keep things cooler during hot weather. And it works. With the cross ventilation from the smaller side windows, we get so much air and light you feel like you're outside. For that matter, it's even better because the screens keep out the flies and mosquitoes."

"And the table under the windows is long and narrow and faces the lake so we can see it from wherever we sit!" I'm sure Uncle Carl knows how happy this makes me as I can tell by the smile on his face.

Still curious, I enter the next room that is about the same size. Grandma has her back to me and is lifting a round cast iron cover from the top of the black iron stove to add wood and crumpled newspaper to the empty hole. The stove is like the one in Grandma's house in Duluth except that it's smaller. She tells me she had this stove before Grandpa got her the new one. "It's still mighty serviceable," she says and bakes wonderful bread.

"Are you making a fire, Grandma?"

"I sure am, dear. These rooms have been closed so long that we need to chase away the dampness."

A small wooden table and a few cupboards are near the stove, and two double beds and an oversized crib are on the opposite end of the room. I wonder if Tommy sleeps in the crib. If he does, it might be big, but pretty soon he'll be even bigger.

"I'll bet lots of people can sleep in this cabin."

"My, yes," Grandma agrees. "The davenport in the other room opens to sleep two people. And did you see the daybed in the corner? That sleeps two people."

They hang blankets on the line to beat winter dust from them, then finish the cleaning and wash dishes in one pan and pour boiling water into another to rinse off any soap.

"Maggie, I need your help in drying the dishes," Aunt Marie says. "Wash your hands first."

"Where?" I ask. Auntie points to a washbasin on a round table near the front entrance.

"But there's no water in it."

Auntie Marie sighs. "Maggie, use your head. You know drinking water must be carried from the Thorngren farm, but we can't possibly carry enough water from there to wash dishes and ourselves. So where do you suppose we get water for the washbasin?"

Boy, I'd better get this right. "From the lake?"

"That's right."

Whew, I think to myself.

"Drinking and cooking water are in the kitchen," she tells me. We keep the lake water in the pail right over there by the washbasin. Be sure you don't get them confused because you don't want to drink lake water. Use the dipper in the pail to put water in the basin."

Living here isn't as easy as it is in Duluth, but I sure can get used to this in a hurry—especially now that I've met Joanna.

Chapter 17

An Emotional Explosion

Jenny

It's dark as Paul and I drive along Lake Michigan, and though it's January, the roads are clear of ice and snow. Few cars pass on this gloomy evening that doesn't regain momentum until a full moon occasionally weaves in and out of a cluster of clouds.

He called earlier to apologize for being late and to explain he was obligated to have a working dinner with an important client before he could join me. Because our evening was cut short, I wasn't surprised when he lost no time in asking me, "Did I win or lose the bet?"

"No one won or lost," I tell him. He appears mystified, which doesn't surprise me.

"Actually, when I arrived for work, Mr. Schumaker didn't seem to be at all upset with me, so I got on with my task of cooking and serving the family that now includes one wife and a mother-in-law. Oh, Paul, you've never seen such a pathetic scene. Mrs. Schumaker can't hold her head up and appears to be lost in a world that doesn't allow anyone to penetrate it."

He shakes his head sympathetically before I add, "I might not have been fired for deserting them at Christmas, but I quit my job a few days later."

His expression changes to one of surprise and bewilderment. "Quit your job?" he says when he recovers. "But why, Jenny? That doesn't sound like you."

As I continue to tell my story, Paul's mood changes, this time to hostility. "That lousy bastard." he states infuriated until he stops abruptly to study me. "Oh, I'm sorry, Jenny. I didn't mean to lose my temper. This certainly wasn't brilliant on his part. From your first description of him, I presumed he was an intelligent fellow, but what he did was make an absolute idiot out of himself."

Paul turns into a rest stop where he stops the car and turns off the motor. "It's such a mild evening that we shouldn't freeze if we stop for a few minutes. We've got a few things to settle, my dear. You do not have a job, and the way I see it, I've won the bet. And you need money to last until you find employment."

"But, Paul, I voluntarily quit my job."

"Yes, but the result is the same. If you hadn't quit after what happened, I wouldn't offer you a cent. You did the right thing, Jenny, and I'm more than happy to pay my bet."

"Thanks," I tell him. To show my appreciation, I reach over to pull his head toward me so I can kiss him on the cheek. Unexpectedly he must have turned toward me at the same time causing our lips to touch ever so lightly. When the first shock is over, I wonder if he's as startled as I am. It most certainly wasn't intentional, but then why did it affect me so deeply that I now feel weak and breathless. This is ridiculous, I tell myself. I know I'm an incurable romantic, but now I sense danger signs flashing in my head.

I observe him studying me with eyes that pierce my very being. This could progress to thin ice, but I'm only too aware that even if Paul isn't married, I most certainly am, so taking this further isn't right. Then other thoughts take over. Was what I experienced in my marriage to Jon a true marriage? With Jonathan, I'd never felt anything like this. Oh, Jenny, I sigh and silently ask myself, "Is this but an excuse for your behavior?" Somehow I can't help but berate myself.

"Paul, I'm so sorry."

He sits back, staring at the darkened sky. "Why should you be?" He smiles at me and says, "Apparently you meant it to be but a kiss of appreciation, so it was but an accident and a very pleasant one at that." Just like Paul to take the sting out of this and set me free again.

"We both know Jonathan is sitting in a correction center and deserves my loyalty, and I'm ready to give him that. I certainly wouldn't want you to think I meant anything disloyal especially since you've been such a good friend."

There's a slight pause until Paul reaches for the key and starts the motor without a word. He turns the car in the direction of the city, and I sit back somewhat baffled. Did I say something wrong? Is he angry with me? It is some time before he speaks, and his next words startle me.

"Let me ask you a question, Jenny. What if Jonathan wasn't faithful to you?" *What a strange comment, I think to myself.* As I ponder that, I become curious—what if?

"Should I have reason to believe he wasn't?" I ask. A cold sensation is erupting inside me, and it certainly isn't the weather.

"Tell me, Paul. Do you know something I don't?"

Silence hangs between us like a rigid curtain. He drives on. The longer the delay, the more the thought sinks in deeper so that I become totally suspicious. Bitterness follows.

When I speak again, my voice surprises even me, denoting shocking strength. "Paul," I say, as anger unveils itself in my voice. "For heaven's sake, pull over somewhere, anywhere so we can finish this conversation."

I clasp my fingers to my forehead as if the pressure might tear the ghastly thoughts from my head. Have I been a blind fool? I look up only when I perceive the car drawing to a stop. Breathing heavily, I turn to see where we are and observe that houses are lined up on both sides of the street like servants standing at attention. A glance in the rearview mirror tells me we are but a short distance from the highway. Paul speaks first.

"Let's not have any misunderstanding, Jenny, because I'm not speaking about myself now. But in my opinion, Jonathan doesn't deserve your closing the door on either leaving him or experiencing any future relationships. I'm sorry to add any more pain to what you've already experienced, but maybe it's best to get this out into the open. I most certainly am not betraying any confidentiality between my client and myself when I tell you this, and I'll explain that to you in a moment."

He hesitates before continuing then speaks slowly and distinctly. "But do you truly want to know, Jenny, since this might bring more pain? Be sure now."

"This will eat at me if I don't know where you're coming from." I nod yes and then add with determination, "I most certainly do want to know."

A professional moment rests between us as if he were trying to find the least hurtful words. Finally Paul seems ready and turns toward me. "The fact is my sister heard rumors that were unfortunately engulfing Laurel Hill about an affair between Jonathan and some woman. She thought she knew the female in this case and abruptly confronted her with the hearsay. I won't divulge her name but was told she broke down and confessed the entire story to my sister Eileen since they were dear friends. She then used my sister's shoulder to cry on. It wasn't long before the two guilty parties who had both broken their marriage vows decided it was too risky to continue their relationship.

"Fortunately for Eileen's friend, Jonathan lost his position at the bank soon after that. Jenny, I'm definitely not suggesting the affair had anything to do with Jonathan being fired. That definitely isn't true." He paused and without knowing it answered my next question. "I'm not sure if they've completely broken off their relationship, but I've heard nothing further since. From what Eileen told me, her friend seemed to pull herself together and no longer said anything further about Jonathan to her."

I sit stunned, angry, and resentful. "Would you forgive me, Paul, if I ask to be taken back to Ruth's now? I'm fighting such intense feelings that I'm afraid I'd be bad company the rest of the evening."

He agrees only if I promise to meet him again in three weeks when he has another meeting in Milwaukee. He pulls an envelope out of his pocket and hands it to me. "I came prepared to pay my bet. Please accept this for now, Jenny, and we'll talk more the first of next month. At least this will give you something to live on in the meantime."

As we approach Ruth and Cliff's apartment, he reaches for my hand again. I experience his strength that is not chiseled from power. Paul's strength is a medley of endurance and kindness, something unknown to me until now. "You're a good friend, Paul." I tell him.

As he opens the door about to walk around to help me out, I stop him.

"Please stay in the car. It will be easier this way." I slip out of the automobile and head for Ruth's apartment without looking back.

Chapter 18

Ruth's Heartache

Jenny

This time it isn't easy to find another assignment. Dr. Sutherland was once again helpful but warned me this is an exceptional position, a dream job, and thus will draw a huge number of women who will request interviews. The Allans own a home in town and a fashionable summer home on a secluded lake about thirty miles north of Milwaukee. Mr. Allan is a wealthy man and able to pay a handsome salary. The only assignment for this employee is the care of their four-year-old daughter, Shirley.

I tell Dr. Sutherland that I would at least like to talk to Mrs. Allan to see if there is a possibility of being hired. No one has any idea how anxious I am to return the money to Paul even if he says he won't take it, and I cannot live with myself if I don't repay that money. These days, when I'm not out looking for a job, I spend my extra time helping Ruth with the cooking, cleaning, and caring for Becky. We have shared many experiences and beliefs, but as I reflect on it, I'm the one who has done most of the sharing. Ruth hasn't been one to talk about herself and that certainly wasn't the case when she was a young girl. Something has changed her. But what?

As I approach the apartment tonight, I feel somewhat relieved as this afternoon I had an encouraging interview with Mrs. Allan. But when I walk in, I'm faced with an unforeseen turn of events. Ruth turns to face me and I notice her eyes are red and she barely greets me before she turns away. After I change into my housedress, I reenter the kitchen and find Ruth looking out the window. There are only two place settings and no sign of Cliff. Becky was profoundly excited this morning when she informed me that she's been invited next door to Jane's birthday party and has been asked to stay for supper as well.

The heat is on under the leftovers, so I stir the carved pot roast in gravy and check the vegetables. Everything is ready to sit down at the table.

"Ruth, supper is ready. Isn't Cliff going to join us tonight?" There is but a quick answer—"No."

No? Why did she answer so abruptly? "I'll fill the serving bowls," I tell her, "and everything will be on the table in no time."

Silence again. But soon Ruth trudges to the table. We eat without conversation, and that's something I haven't experienced since I arrived in Milwaukee. I can't stand this "quiet noise" any longer.

"Ruth, I can tell something is bothering you. I'm always pouring out my heart to you, but you seldom share anything with me except memories of when we were children. Please, dear, won't you tell me what's wrong?"

Again there is silence for a short time until Ruth says, "Guess I can't keep this to myself, but it will no doubt come as a bombshell to you. Let's wait until we finish eating. I'll tell you what it is over dessert." It isn't long before her story rolls out like tumbleweeds blowing over desert sand.

"Jenny, I'm upset because I had a fierce argument with Cliff. I threw him out."

Did I hear her right? "But why, Ruth? What did he do?"

"When I got home from shopping today, I found that the despicable man I married had opened a box of my letters. They were strewn all over the floor, torn into bits until completely destroyed. Perhaps he's always been suspicious of why I kept that box taped with a pink ribbon tied around it, but why couldn't he have asked me what was in it? I would have told him, but he never seemed interested. He was upset today about losing his job and had a little too much to drink. Apparently his curiosity got the better of him."

"Letters? What letters?"

"'What letters *were* they is more like it." Ruth looks at me and shrugs her shoulders. "Guess I'd better start at the beginning.

"Remember after we graduated from high school that I went away to college? Your folks didn't have the money to send you, and I was lost without you. We'd done everything together, and I was so lonely that I threw myself into my studies. All I wanted was to learn, learn, and keep learning. I specifically appreciated the English class, but not only for the knowledge I gained but because I joined many of the girls in being fascinated with our handsome professor. He was young, about six feet tall, thin, and had a magnificent head of dark, wavy hair. The girls would say, "Wish I could cook for him. I'd make nothing but fattening foods because he's so thin he almost looks sick."

Ruth sighed deeply, took another bite of her cake, and continued. "Before the semester was over, who do you suppose the professor was attracted to?"

I point my finger at her.

"Yes, but it wasn't because I'm some great beauty. He believed I was high-spirited, fun, and a good student. That's what he wanted in a woman. I know it was definitely against the rules of a no student/teacher relationship. But he wasn't married, and we were tired of the stupid rules so we began seeing each other after class. Naturally we were most discreet because he could lose his job if anyone reported having seen us together. In the spring when the blossoms were on the trees and the air was scented with their fragrance, one thing led to another and . . . well, I suppose you'd say we got carried away. We talked about marriage but made no plans. Before long I realized that I could possibly be pregnant."

The gasp must have come from me, and Ruth stops for a moment. When she continues, I once again have control of myself.

"When classes were over for the semester, Andrew told me he was going home to visit his family. I made an appointment with the doctor, and when my condition was confirmed I was most anxious to tell the future father. I called him at the end of the week when he said he'd be back. I kept calling for days without success, and by then I was extremely worried. What if there's been some disaster like a car accident? Finally I walked to his apartment only to discover he'd moved out. When the landlord told me that, it hit me like a bomb. I asked if he'd left a forwarding address; the answer was no.

"Oh, Jenny," Ruth moans. "I was devastated. Why had he done this without telling me? Was he even telling the truth when he said he loved me? Now I was more angry than upset, and I kept wondering what I should do.

"When I went home to the farm to discuss this with my mother, our plan was that I visit my aunt in Chicago until the baby was born. Then I was to return home so that Mother would raise the baby as her child. Is this making sense to you now? My sister isn't really my sister; Dolores is my oldest daughter. Thank heavens, my mother helped me because you know what people would have said about me having a baby without being married. I would have been one of "those" women.

"I never did go back to college. Andrew wasn't teaching, and no one was telling the class why. What had happened?

"Then I learned his sister Jeanie was working at the University of Minnesota. When I had the opportunity to search for her, I was successful, and Jeanie's kindness impressed me tremendously. She said her brother was in a tuberculosis sanitarium in Alga, Minnesota. Tears flooded her eyes when she told me she'd learned recently that he might have but a short time to live. That horrifying news sent chills down my spine and I panicked. I told her about the baby, and I could see by the sympathetic expression in her eyes that she understood the anguish. Jeanie assured me she would make the trip with me if I wanted to visit him. "He should know this," she said.

Ruth's voice cracked at this point, and I wondered if she could go on. But Ruth is a strong woman, and after taking a deep breath and letting out a huge sigh, she was able to continue.

"Jeanie and I made the trip to Alga. When Andrew learned I was pregnant at the time he left for the sanitarium, he assured me he would never have left without me if he'd known this. He only wanted to protect me and thought it would be easier for both of us the way he handled it. Andrew told me one of his greatest weaknesses is that he hates good-byes.

"He apologized often for not involving me, Jenny. Would I marry him now? He said he loved me dearly and hadn't been able to think of much else since the last time we saw one other.

"We were married as soon as we could get a license and engage a minister. The ceremony was held in his hospital room, and Jeanie and a favorite nurse were witnesses. The staff provided a lovely cake, and they all stopped by to congratulate and hug us. I had a new sister-in-law and embraced her with love when she had to say goodbye. She'd been offered a ride back to Minneapolis if she could leave promptly, and since it was important that she get back to work, she accepted the kind offer. I stayed with Andrew almost a week, and we talked about everything that had happened to us since we'd been apart. He asked me to please send him pictures of the baby.

"His letters were treasures. Andrew wrote touching messages daily that must have exhausted him for he was exceptionally weak. I sent him pictures of his baby daughter. He said we both meant everything to him and had given him tremendous joy. I tied the dispatches with pink satin ribbon so Dolores could read them when she was older. Andrew died one month after we were married."

I sit very still and feel like I've been hit with a flying rock. What Ruth must have gone through keeping this to herself all this time.

I watch her rise from the table and head for the stove. I quickly follow her and turn her around to face me. I place my arms around my dear cousin and give her a warm hug that's from my heart. She's so precious to me and quivers as I hold her but does not cry. Instead she accepts my gift of love.

Ruth squeezes my hand as if to say "thanks" and then reaches for the coffee pot. When she fills our cups once again, we both return to the table.

"You've been here for me so many times, Ruth, and you've let me pour out my heart to you and share my problems. It's helped me more than I can tell you. Please remember that I'm here for you too, and I know from experience how much it helps to talk over the important things that happen to us.

"I'm so sorry," I tell her. "To lose something as precious as those irreplaceable letters must be agony. You told me Cliff lost his job, but what will you do if he doesn't find employment soon so he can at least give you support money for Becky?"

Ruth brightens as she tells me, "This might seem strange—almost as if the good Lord was preparing me for facing this agonizing experience with Cliff. Fortunately I recently talked to the woman who's been setting my hair. She's the owner, and I added how interested I was in learning to be a hairdresser. I explained that I didn't have the money to learn the profession, so my dream job would never materialize.

"Do you know what she told me? She said that if I honestly feel that deeply about learning that she'd teach me the ropes and we'd make a bargain. While learning the business, my salary would be minimal, but when I knew what I was doing and was able to please the customers, my earnings would be up to speed. It was as if a miracle was spread out before me. I most certainly intended to tell you this but was waiting to make some progress before surprising you.

"Jenny, would you be willing to take care of Becky until you find a new assignment? My gracious neighbor will care for her then and said she can really use the money I offered to pay. Her wages will increase when my salary grows. I'd be willing to pay you something as well until you can locate a job."

Her statement was like a wake-up call for me. Had I forgotten that God is our loving father and will always help us if we but ask Him? I need Him too. Now and always.

"I'll be more than happy to care for the little pumpkin until I find another job. But I'll accept no money because I'm family, remember? It's so nice of your neighbor to offer her help too. She is a caring woman.

"So it seems you have this worked out. I do have one question though. Are you sure you want to take these steps, Ruth? Is it a divorce you want?"

"I'm positive, Jenny. I do want a divorce. I know it won't be easy, but I can't live with a drunken, jealous man who continually neglects me. Thank goodness, you've been here for company because lately if he wasn't working late, he was at a lodge meeting or used that as an excuse.

Chapter 19

Which Road Do I Take?

Jenny

I open Marie's letter first. When I reach the end, I give a sigh of relief because all is well. Maggie rode to the lake with the family when they prepared the lake cottage for summer occupancy. She'd been enchanted with the small cabin and the surrounding area especially when a girl named Joanna befriended her. I know it's important for most of us to have friends, but it's vital for Maggie.

I sense the brain power of my sister Marie accelerating as she writes that she has made an agenda for the summer. When the school year ends, Mother will care for Tommy and Maggie at the lake cottage during the week, and she and Carl will join them Friday after work to spend the weekend. They'll bring food and clean clothes and gather the soiled clothing to take back to town to be washed. The agenda has been set in motion, and everyone is looking forward to summer.

Overjoyed at the good news, I set the letter aside and consider the next envelope. My eagerness to open it surprises me.

I've tried to convince myself Paul doesn't mean much to me, but I know I've been carried away by his personality and the fun we have together. I'm unsteady as I open his letter.

Relief follows as I gaze at a simple "I will be in Milwaukee on . . ." and nothing further is said beyond giving me the date he plans to be here. I'm only too aware that I shouldn't be seeing him at all, but he is a good friend and I cannot hurt him by refusing his invitation. The following week when Paul calls at Ruth's, I'm ready. I didn't write to confirm the meeting but left it dangling, awaiting fate's decision.

In case he takes me to Rudolphs again, I will wear an alluring pink dress selected from the few clothes I have left from my life in Upper Michigan. I know the dress will blend with the decor.

I'm delighted when Paul does take me to Rudolphs. Everything is as elegant as I remember. I had been so nervous on that first visit that I could barely eat. Tonight I'm relaxed, comfortable in Paul's presence, and relishing the steak I ordered. As we dance, I'm content and light on my feet. His arms hold me gently, and I float to the music especially the one they'd played the first time we danced together. The music and words are now familiar.

> So kiss me, my sweet,
> And so let us part,
> And when I grow too old to dream,
> That kiss will live in my heart.

"At first I didn't sense it, but it's actually a sad song," Paul comments. As if the orchestra hears his words, a more cheerful melody bursts forth as we slither around tables to reach the one we'd been assigned.

When I first told Paul I must go with the Allan family to their summer home until September, he understood why it would be complicated for him to visit me during that time. I would have no specific "days off" but would be given extended time later in the year. Now he asks the difficult question.

"Do you think we could reconsider our plans not to see each other this summer?" he asks. "I could pick you up every three weeks, and we could head for Milwaukee for the day only if you'd enjoy that. There are movies to see, restaurants to visit, and it would help pass the summer months and keep them from dragging," he suggests.

"Let me see what I can do," I tell him. "Yes, I would like that."

I wish I could tell him what Ruth had recently confided to me, but I don't have her permission. For now, I know I must tell him my fears as difficult as that might be.

"I know I'm taking a chance changing my mind about this, Paul, because if someone should misconstrue our friendly relationship as a scandal, I could be in danger of losing my children. They're my life, and I miss them so intensely that there isn't a day that passes that I don't think about them and yearn to see them."

At that moment, the waiter approaches our table and asks if we'd like dessert. I slowly nod my head, and Paul says, "Fill our coffee cups once again and then bring me the check."

The waiter departs and Paul covers my hand with his. From the serious expression on his face, I fear what he might say.

"Jenny, I'm only too aware of how much you adore your children, and that's only one of the reasons I admire you so much. I wouldn't continue our meetings if I believed there was any danger in it or had hope you and Jonathan could ever make a true marriage. I fear there's been too much pain already. Marriage should be a joy and filled with a desire to share life. That demands true love and willingness to put the other person first above your own desires. It can't be based on staying married for the children's sake and that alone which isn't fair even to them. You need to know in your heart that you can forgive him and rebuild your marriage. Jonathan must be sure you're the only woman for him and therefore want to be faithful to you or it isn't worth the effort. Of course, we can't be sure of any of this, but does it mean we can't continue to see each other on a friendly basis?"

"And what if Jon and I, in trying to renew our rocky marriage, find it doesn't work?" I ask.

He squeezes my hand tightly. "If you two can't make it and want a divorce, visitation rights can be worked out. Without a doubt, it will take time for you both to go through this entire procedure, and it won't be easy."

Never before has anyone treated me with more consideration and understanding. We enjoy each other, laugh together, respect each other, and take pleasure in so many of the same things. I know he's the best male friend I've ever had. Perhaps

I live in too much fear and should reconsider enjoying our last summer.

"I can see something is still bothering you, Jenny. What is it?"

"It's what I'll have to go through to get a divorce that disturbs me. I've always feared Jonathan and have always done whatever he says. Maybe I have to build on the friendship you and I enjoy to realize I'm a person worth caring about. One more thing. Few people get a divorce, and if they do, everyone looks down on them as if they have claws instead of hands."

Paul shakes his head. "So folks live a life of hell so people won't think the worst of them? If you see no hope ahead, Jenny, you must realize that you are a much stronger person than you realize. Think about this. Is it really so important what people think?"

Now I can clearly see why Paul is a lawyer. I'd most definitely always believed it's important what people think of me. But was I right? Maybe Jonathan would even like his freedom from me. Marrying someone who is interested in amateur radio, bowling, baseball, football, and all other sports or even one sport for that matter could possibly bring him more happiness than living with me when I find all these things uninteresting and a waste of time. I reflect now that I should have realized this before I married Jon, but then he's never been honest with me either as to what he truly enjoys. We need to communicate with honesty and tell each other what we really believe.

"I'll help all I can while you're still in Milwaukee," Paul says. "This is probably a good time to tell you that Jonathan's cousin George and I have had indications we might be successful getting Jon's sentence shortened. It looks now as if we might get the number of years of service cut to three instead of five. If so, a little over a year from now Jonathan will be a free man."

A year? Will I be ready? I'm sure talking this over with Jon will be a nightmare for some time. One thing I realize now is that I must live through this experience with him whether I like it or not. But is there really hope of a happier life for me?

I look at Paul with new eyes. "I see now that I do need your help to become stronger and do the right thing for all of us. Thanks, dear friend, and I would truly appreciate your help throughout the summer months. You can reach me through Ruth or general delivery."

Chapter 20

Glowing Cabin Days

Maggie

The screen door slams behind me, and I jump. I hang my dripping raincoat on a front porch hook and remove my wet shoes so they won't track up the floor. If I forget, I must clean up the mess myself.

"Grandma, do you know I love everything about being here more than in Duluth except when it rains and I have to run to the outhouse?" A giggle escapes before I can say, "It's no fun to go to that smelly old place anytime, but at least today I didn't see any spiders, which you probably have already figured out 'cause I didn't scream. I just hate those little guys."

It's been raining since yesterday, and I feel like a prisoner, having to stay indoors with no swimming with friends or hiking with Joanna to Bailey to get the groceries needed by Grandma or Mrs. Kelly. Grandma is so nice and always gives me a nickel to buy my favorite candy bar, which is a huge Milky Way to share with Joanna. Today I'd even be thankful to walk to the mailbox with anyone whose turn it is to pick up the mail if only this stupid rain stops.

"Magg-eeee, come play old maid with me." *Fooey*, I think to myself. Every time it rains, Tommy wants to play cards with me. He has his own special way to shuffle the deck, and when the cards fly up in the air, he knows he has to pick them off the floor. Still he keeps doing it. He gets so restless in this weather and wants my attention all the time, and the worst part is that he wants to win all the time. He needs to learn that isn't the way it happens in real life. I'd much rather play 500 Rummy with Grandma Nelly, but I've learned that you can't always have what you want.

One neat thing about my staying indoors is that I have time to visit with Grandma Nelly. Yesterday when I was wiping a saucer, it accidentally flew out of my hand only to crash and break into little pieces. I was scared stiff that Grandma would be mad, but she wasn't 'cause she said she knew I didn't do it on purpose. Then she told me how last year she broke a treasured heart-shaped crystal vase that cousin Louisa in Norway had given her for a wedding present. She didn't mean to break it; it just happened.

"Did you cry?"

"No, honey," Grandma says before she explains something very important for me to learn. "I've lived a long time, and I've learned much. I dearly loved that gift, but I had to let it go as the pieces could never fit back together." She then told me she'd always love and cherish the vase the way it was when it was whole. "When something that important breaks, you never really lose it, dear."

Grandma Nelly is so smart. When she talks to me like that, it's a present all by itself because she makes me feel grown up. What she said is a gift too.

When Mama left, I broke in little pieces just like that vase. At first, the pieces tried to get back together, but they couldn't. I thought Mama would have to be here to get me pieced together like when you patch with glue, but it started without her.

It began when Aunt Marie believed me when I was falsely accused of writing on the school bathroom walls. It helped more than anything when Mama came home for Christmas. But what really made the pieces fit solid was when Grandma said she'd care for Tommy and me here at the cabin during the summer months. It's been such a swell vacation with Joanna as my friend, her sisters to teach me to swim, all of us attending the Kayler Player performances in Bailey where we'd sit on benches and boo the bad guys and cheer the good ones, and of course, there was our writing club. We met weekly to vote on the best story. One of the Kelly kids would usually win, but I never knew if it was because my stories weren't good or if they felt they should be loyal to their sisters and brothers. I didn't really care because it was such fun to listen to them read, and once I did win. If their chores were done, evenings we'd get together in their front yard to play games like "New York, what's your trade, lemonade, give-me-some."

"Oh, Grandma, look. I think the rain is stopping and here comes Joanna, so it must be her turn to walk to the mailbox. Can I go with her? Please, Grandma, pretty please with sugar on it?"

My friend Joanna and I are fast walkers so it doesn't take us long to reach the mailboxes. Soon we see the mailman drive up, stop his car, hang out the window, and then put mail into each of four boxes that belong to nearby families. He drives off, but when we walk to the Kelly mailbox, we find nothing but the daily newspaper. The mailbox is near the Gorge family farm, and Joanna tells me they don't mind if we use their swing to sit in while we look at the funnies. We wiggle into it to get comfortable while we cackle at Jiggs and Maggie, laugh at Tillie the Toiler, and just adore Little Orphan Annie. There's a whole page of funnies, and Joanna and I take turns reading them aloud.

Hiking back, Joanna tells me you never know what surprises the mailman will bring us. "The best is in the middle of summer," she says, "when the Montgomery Ward and Sears Roebuck catalogs come. We all scramble to pick out our school clothes."

"You send for them in the mail?"

"Sure. There's not much to choose from in the stores of a small town like Bailey. We study the catalog pictures and make choices of what we want most of all even if Ma and Pa can't afford it. Usually we must choose something less expensive and know we must be content with that. The girls usually get one kinda good dress and two cheaper ones. The boys get new overalls and a warm shirt. When we're finished with the catalogs, they end up in the outhouse."

"The outhouse? Why would you put them there?"

"We can't afford to buy toilet paper so it's used for that."

Oh my goodness, and I try hard to quickly think of something else to say.

"Joanna, may I put a letter to my mother in your mailbox for the postman to pick up?" I gotta tell her how much our family will love this place. I can see it now where Daddy will work in town and make money while Mama and Grandma take care of us kids.

"Sure you can write her letters and mail them here," Joanna says. "And if you need stamps, you can buy them at the post office in Bailey on our next trip to town. You can even get penny postcards."

"Penny postcards? What are penny postcards?"

"You don't know? That's a card where you have one side to write a message before turning it over to write the address on the other side. That costs only a penny while a stamp costs three cents, so you see it's cheaper to write post cards."

"Can Mama send mail for me to your mailbox?"

"Sure," she tells me and says she'll write down her mailbox address when she gets home so I can send it to my mother. We walk in silence for a while as we pass the Thorngren fields that have been freshly cut. It smells so good.

"Maggie, after I do my chores this afternoon, can you go swimming with me?"

"I'll ask Grandma. She makes Tommy and me take an hour nap after lunch though. She says that's so we won't get stomach cramps and drown when we swim. I hate that because I never sleep and time goes so darned slow."

When Joanna's mother settles on a chair, she covers the whole seat while a portion of her overweight body spills over the edge on both sides. We hardly ever see Mr. Kelly who works in town plus doing what Mrs. Kelly calls overseeing the work on the farm where their older children have important duties and chores to do. The glimpses I've had of Joanna's father showed a true Irishman with fiery red hair and a matching bushy mustache that curls at the corners of his mouth. He looks short and skinny especially when he walks next to his tall and chubby wife.

Grandma says the Kellys are the most kind and generous people she knows. I know that's true because Mrs. Kelly promised me that she'll plant a long row of wax string beans in her vegetable garden next spring just for me. First, though, I have to promise her to weed my row of beans and pick them often to take to Grandma to cook. This made me so happy because I'd helped her weed her garden and loved it. I betcha I enjoy wax beans as much as Grandma does especially when she makes her delicious cream sauce to pour over them. They're absolutely heavenly, and next year, I can have all I want. Today Mrs. Kelly brought Grandma some rhubarb, radishes, and roses from her garden. I really like this kind lady who is tall with light brown hair that's short and straight. Her gray dress with red trim hangs loose, and Joanna says her mother sews their everyday summer dresses from old feed sacks that have different patterns on them.

When I get back from my walk with Joanna, the ladies are playing 500 Rummy, so I quietly get behind Grandma to see what she has in her hand and then tiptoe away. I've been taught to say nothing so I don't let anyone know what cards she has, and Grandma Nelly says I must wear a "poker face."

Joanna and I go outside to visit. She tells me her mother is strict, but I've never noticed that. Joanna says all of us kids must do chores before they're released for free time. Ma's rule is "First work and then play." She smiles and adds, "But when you visit from Duluth, I get a little extra time off." I'm so glad. It shows on Joanna's face that she's serious when she explains, "When Ma tells us how important it is that we all do our share, we do it."

When I tell this to Grandma, she says that Mrs. Kelly knows how to raise children to be responsible citizens. We don't have as many chores at the cabin as the Kellys do, but Grandma tells me I must help to keep the cottage clean. I sweep every day, make beds, and yesterday I helped her by heating the irons on the hot stove to press the dampened handkerchiefs and pillow cases. That was lots of fun, and I was so proud. We have no icebox at the cabin, so Grandma teaches me to take food that can spoil to a place where it can last longer. She tells me that before he moved to Montana, Grandpa dug this hole deep into the earth so we can safely guide food in to keep it cold. I ask if he learned this in Norway, and Grandma says yes. Then she shows me how to reach far down to put food in the lowest possible place. I'm in charge of this whenever she asks me. I know it's a big responsibility, but I can do it to prove to Grandma and Auntie Marie how helpful I can be.

My favorite fun thing at the cabin is swimming and floating on those inner tubes that Uncle Carl makes for Tommy and me. When one of the tires on his car goes flat, he removes the innertube for patching. When it's ready, he tests it in the lake to make sure it floats. If it does, I slip in to sit in the doughnut hole with my legs dangling over the side. If the wind is blowing strong enough, it moves me along as if I'm a sailboat and gives me an absolutely swell feeling. Auntie Marie gave Tommy and me rubber bathing slippers that sure do help my tender feet that hurt when I walk on the small rocks that keep washing ashore. Auntie says my feeble feet are that way because I always walk with my shoes on. There's a reason for that. When I saw how Joanna's brother Pat cut his feet when he was walking barefoot, I made up my mind that wasn't for me. I saw icky picky blood all over the ground. Now I learn from Uncle Carl that there's something else the rubber slippers are good for and that's to protect our feet from bloodsuckers.

"Bloodsuckers?" I scream. "What are they? I don't like that name, Uncle Carl. Do they suck blood out of you?"

He explains that bloodsuckers are really small leeches, and unfortunately, we do have some little ones along the shoreline.

"Golly, Uncle Carl, I'm scared of spiders and other bugs, and now I have this to worry about?"

He pulls up a chair to face me. "I didn't mean to frighten you, child." I listen real good as he tells me bloodsuckers are flat, black creatures—a small worm-like animal that won't hurt you unless you disturb it. If you do, it wiggles and swells. They usually latch on to fish but occasionally find their way near shore to settle in an undisturbed area to look for human victims.

"We hardly ever notice them because we're usually in our swimming area that is constantly stirred up," he says. "But if you venture into a calm area like the other side of the dock where no one goes, they could be in big bunches. If you aren't wearing something on your feet, they could latch onto your toes."

I ask him once again, "But do they really suck blood out of your feet?"

"If they stay on you long enough." He reaches for my hand, probably to try to calm me.

"There is a solution, Maggie."

"A solution? Does that mean we can do something about them? Save me, Uncle Carl. What is it?"

"If you ever get one on your toe, ask your Grandma to sprinkle salt on the friendly little guy and he'll wiggle away because they certainly don't like salt."

Boy, you can be sure I'll have plenty of salt nearby when I swim. I must remember to thank Auntie Marie again for the truly *necessary* gift of the bathing slippers.

There's no grandfather clock here to strike the hours, so the summer rule is that bedtime comes with the setting of the sun. It's almost time to go back to school for the winter months, so the sun sets earlier now. While I'm still here, Joanna has the treat of getting out of late chores so she can meet me on the vacant lot that separates our cottage from the road that leads to her farm. This is a special time when we watch the sun that's many times a giant ball of fire when it nears the horizon.

Tonight I hurry to wipe dishes and put them away. I'm afraid I'm late, but Joanna isn't here yet. I settle in a comfortable spot on the soft grass and hope she comes soon.

While I wait, I see the sky change before my eyes. I scan the horizon and watch streaks of clouds stretch over the dark blue space. God blows them into position as only He knows where they belong. Mama told me that. I hold my breath as I see His latest masterpiece when the colors of the clouds change. The air is warm and sweet-smelling, and I hear the chirping of crickets, croaking of frogs, and gentle waves tickling the shore.

Here comes Joanna skipping down the road to join me as we share the most beautiful sight in the world. We're spellbound as we make memories.

Chapter 21

Changes

Jenny

Ruth hands me the mirror so I can examine my new hairdo.

"So, what do you think?" she asks.

I check all sides of my head. "Ruth, it's lovely. Fran was right when she said you have a knack for making a woman look special. Is this really me?"

"You bet it is. Fran has been a great instructor." Ruth removes her smock. "Well, I'm done for the day. Want to head back to the apartment?"

"By all means," I tell her. "It's so good to have a few free days. It's almost Christmas, and I'm looking forward to trimming the tree tonight just like in the old days.

We climb the familiar staircase and stop at the neighbor's door to pick up Becky. When the little one sees who is with her mother, she reaches out for me and gives me an energetic hug, then grasps my hand as we follow Ruth into her kitchen.

"Becky," I say, studying her. "You've grown so much since I last saw you. You'll be as big as your mother soon." The four-year-old grins and points to her mother.

"She's a giant," Becky jokes with a giggle.

"You'll catch up to her one of these days especially if you eat a lot of carrots. Then you'll grow like a weed."

The child's mouth opens, and she looks at me apparently distressed. "I don't want to be a weed, Aunt Yenny."

"Oh honey, I didn't mean to upset you. I just meant that weeds grow faster than a bunny. You're much too pretty to be a weed."

I'm relieved when I see that I've hit the right note. Becky smiles as she's noticed a pot of carrots boiling on the stove. Now I'm sure she won't fail to eat them.

Ruth has prepared a large pot of "susachut," and I jubilantly cut the tender beef into smaller pieces with my fork. The gravy and onions smother the meat and boiled potatoes. How I enjoy Norwegian food!

After the dishes have been washed and dried, I have the pleasure of putting Becky to bed. She isn't about to release me until she has covered me with hugs and kisses.

Soft music from the little radio on the counter engulfs the kitchen as Ruth and I sit around the table to chat over a cup of tea. What Ruth says next makes my blood run cold.

"There's something I must tell you, Jenny."

I don't like the sound of my cousin's voice for the tone is much too serious.

"The closer Cliff and I get to the date of our divorce, the meaner he gets when he calls me. It's troubling, and the time has come for me to make some changes. I've written Mother and she's invited Becky and me to stay on the farm until I can find a job either in Calgary or some town nearby. I need to put many miles between my soon-to-be 'ex' and my daughter."

I sense Ruth's eyes are watching me to get my reaction. My mind is struggling to grasp all this news and apparently I'm wearing my stone face. When she doesn't get immediate feedback, she continues with "I do feel bad that I'm responsible for your move to Milwaukee, and now I'm the one abandoning you."

"Oh, Ruth," I tell her as I reach for her hand to hold it in mine. "You've got to think of yourself first. I'll be fine and was only momentarily sad to think of you moving away so soon. If I didn't have this great job, it would be much more difficult. Believe me when I say that I'll truly miss you. Not having this time to spend with you will cause me to be very lonely, but my life will be changing soon anyway." These days, my cousin needs me for whatever support I can give her, and I'll always remember the great times we've had together.

"When does Jonathan hope to be released from the corrections center?" Ruth asks. I'd shared the news with her that his sentence might be reduced, so the question doesn't surprise me.

"His hearing comes up the beginning of August. I do hope to return to Duluth before that because I want time to be alone with the children before Jonathan comes home. I'm saving every nickel to make sure that happens. That's why Maggie is satisfied waiting until summer to see me. My target date is the 1st of June. When are you leaving, Ruth?"

"I plan to leave right after the divorce is final. That should be by the end of January."

It's a relief to know I have a job with a place to live and move the remainder of my clothes. As I sort this out, it seems nothing is forever. Then I smile and tell her, "But it's not as if we're both going into obscurity. Duluth and Calgary aren't that far apart, and we can visit each other.

"What I'm grateful for, Ruth, is how close we've become once again. When we were children, we shared everything. After the many years when we didn't see each other, we've had the blessing of this time together. It's been wonderful and certainly a blessing to share so many private experiences that we didn't feel we could discuss with anyone else. What I'm truly sorry about is that you'll be leaving on such a despondent note."

"Oh, I'll survive," Ruth says before she rises and adds, "I'm sure Becky is sound asleep by now, Jenny. Shall we trim that tree?"

Paul is aware that Ruth is leaving Milwaukee, and I'm delighted when he suggests we should take her to dinner soon. “She’s been so kind and understanding that the least we can do is give her a special night out. Will you help with the arrangements, Jenny?”

“If you can possibly stay over another day, we might be able to do it tomorrow night,” I tell him. He assures me he will call the office in the morning.

The next evening as we draw up to the restaurant, Ruth is delighted when she sees Rudolphs’ sign. It’s obvious from the start that Cliff has never taken his wife to anything this elegant.

“The mirrors on the walls and pink color might at first appear feminine,” Paul tells her, “but this is a charming place where any gentleman who truly loves his lady and wants to please her would not care if the decor were masculine or feminine as long as she enjoys it.” I had described the restaurant to Ruth earlier, but nothing I could have said would even come close to its beauty. She had to see this for herself.

We’re shown to a table where my cousin smiles as she confides to Paul that she had never expected anything so grand.

“You deserve it, young lady. You’ve been so kind to us that I had to give you a special going-away dinner. It’s the least I could do.”

We all listen as the waiter explains the evening specials, and I’m quick to order.

“Tonight the salmon appeals to me.” I wink at him as I say, “After all, I’m Norwegian.” Ruth requests the same.

Paul looks disappointed. “Do you, mean that on this special occasion you won’t join me in having Rudolphs’ prime rib special?” She leans toward him and confirms it is truly salmon that appeals to her more than anything else. “After all, I’m Norwegian, too.” He grins and nods in acceptance for he knows when he’s beaten and orders the prime rib for himself. The waiter makes no notations as he memorizes all orders. He serves the coffee and places a basket of bread and rolls before us.

“How soon are you planning to leave, Ruth?”

She accepts the menu as Paul orders coffee with cream for all of us. “I’m about packed,” Ruth tells him. “The moving van will be at our apartment early Monday morning. I don’t believe Becky has any idea what’s going on yet. We’re making a game of it.”

Paul opens his mouth and stares. "That soon?"

"I'm afraid so," she says. "It's due to Cliff and what he's been pulling lately."

"I'm afraid Paul doesn't know what you're talking about, Ruth, as we haven't discussed it. That's a story I believe you should tell him yourself."

"It's no secret, Jenny. You certainly could have told Paul, but since you didn't, I will." She looks up from buttering a roll and begins her near-tragic tale.

"Paul, I was more than hesitant when before Christmas Cliff called and said he had some gifts for Becky. Would we both come for dinner on Christmas Eve? He proceeded to plead saying he wanted her to remember she had a father, and this would make Christmas special for both of them." Ruth stops to look at me. "Jenny knows what a softy I am, and unfortunately I gave in to his wishes."

"The evening started out fine, and he'd actually prepared a fairly decent dinner. That was a surprise to me because he never volunteered to cook when we were together. Becky was thrilled with the small tree her father had decorated for her and was delighted to open the gifts he'd placed under it. After some time, I mentioned going home, but Cliff asked me to put Becky down for a nap so we could visit. I was suspicious and didn't agree especially since he was jiggling the ice in his glass that contained his fourth drink of bootleg liquor. He was getting louder, and when I refused to stay, I could see he was irritated; yet I still hoped he would settle down. Silly me—as if one could count on getting a drunk to straighten out in a single evening. Becky was enjoying her gifts, so I told her she could play while we talked. But what was there to discuss?"

The waiter appears with the soup and a fancy fruit gelatin salad. I suggest Ruth stop her saga to at least enjoy her soup while it's hot.

"Sure, *you* can say that," Paul teases. "You know what comes next."

Ruth looks at me and laughs before saying, "Good suggestion, Jenny" as she takes my tip to give the delectable soup her undivided attention. When we finish and the busboy removes the dishes, Ruth continues.

"I should have guessed what Cliff wanted to discuss as naturally he was trying to change my mind about getting a divorce. He was becoming noisier, and now Becky stopped playing, stared at him, and drew near her father to put her finger to her lips to say, 'Shhhhh, Daddy.'"

Ruth closed her eyes as if she were reliving the scene. "I could see the anger in Cliff's eyes and dreaded the worst, so I got down on my hands and knees and packed Becky's toys before heading for the bedroom to pick up our coats. Cliff was following me, and when I turned and saw him, he threw me onto the bed. I've got a strong arm when I'm pushed too far and hit him where it hurts the most before I struggled to my feet."

Paul closes his eyes, moans, and shakes his head but says nothing.

"It took Cliff a time to get through the pain," Ruth continues, "so I was able to get our coats and leave by way of the front door with Becky minus her toys. She screamed for her presents though I paid no attention since our safety came first. We started down the steps when I heard Cliff let out a strangled cry above Becky's sobbing. He was at the top of the stairs warning, 'Stop or I'll shoot.' I wasn't concerned but kept going because I was sure he had no gun. Then I heard the first shot. My instincts told me to run, so I did while holding tightly to Becky's hand. Cliff fired a total of five shots, but by some miracle, I managed to get to the car safely with only one bullet searing the bottom of my coat.

"I would have driven off but realized that in my haste I'd forgotten my purse that contained my keys. The shots must have sobered Cliff enough to realize what he'd done because he went back inside. Thankfully the neighbors had called the police who were able to get my purse and Becky's toys. I was free to leave after they asked their routine questions.

When Ruth finishes, there's an uncomfortable silence before she asks, "Jenny, do you have anything to add?"

"Not really," I respond, "because I was asleep by the time you got home and knew nothing about what had gone on. But I do remember the next day when I went out to get the newspaper. I was shocked to find the story on the front page.

It was a jolt, and I couldn't wait for you to wake up so I was sure you were both okay."

All three of us at the table sit back as we watch the busboy clear the dishes. The waiter comes shortly thereafter and sets the main course before us. Ruth smiles and says, "This looks fit for a queen." Her story finished, she could now relax and enjoy her meal.

"Did you file charges?" Paul asks.

"No. I was decent to him, except for that one incident, and expect he won't fight me on the divorce after that performance. Furthermore, Becky and I were shaken but not really hurt."

"Ruth, are you adjusting to becoming the single woman that you'll be before long?" Paul asks. But he has to wait for his answer until she pours cream into her coffee and stirs it.

"It's a good thing I've been separated from Cliff for a couple months because I did get somewhat used to not having him around. After what he pulled at Christmas, though, I'm extremely thankful to be alone."

When we finish eating, Paul bends toward me and asks if I mind if he asks Ruth to dance. "By all means, please do. I'm sure she'll love it."

I observe them glide gracefully on the dance floor and once again am reminded of how much Ruth has changed. The nightmare of the past few months has whittled ten pounds from her tall body, making her appear less dowdy. Being a hair stylist came with the bonus that others would occasionally work on her hair. They've come up with a stylish cut that flatters her. When you place a jewel in its proper setting, its brilliance multiplies.

The evening is over much too soon. As we drop Ruth off at the entrance to her apartment, I encourage her to retire early with the promise I'll help her pack in the morning as I have the weekend off. Paul accepts Ruth's thanks for a captivating evening, and he's every bit as sincere when he thanks her once again for her kindness.

The evening is clear and crisp as Paul and I drive along the lakeshore. We discuss the evening's events, and he says,

“She’ll be fine now. No need to worry. The one I’m concerned about is you, dear. Ruth has been your safe harbor, and now that ship is about to pull anchor and sail off.”

“I agree that Ruth will be fine, but so will I. I’ll continue to accumulate my days off that I can take later. If there’s no opportunity to do that, I’m sure when I leave for Duluth that I’ll be compensated for the time I’ve accrued. One thing I’m sure of is that Mrs. Allan will be fair.”

“Does she know yet that you’re planning to leave in a few months?”

“Not yet. I’ll tell her when it’s closer to the time I plan to leave.” A sadness comes over me as I realize how much I’ve loved this job. “Mrs. Allan will have plenty of time to hire someone to take my place. She deserves that.”

Chapter 22

The Picnic

Jenny

Ruth left for her mother's farm over two months ago, and since then, I've had nothing I've wanted to do with my days off. When Mrs. Allan sees that I have no desire to claim the time I've earned, she suggests I accumulate my free hours to make my paycheck larger when I leave for Duluth.

But things change. Now I have two unexpected requests. The first is not something I want to do, but I can't see how I can get out of it. My longtime friend Gloria writes from her home in Duluth to ask me to accompany her to the Illinois correction center where Jonathan is being held because her brother has been sent to the same facility. What has Gus done now? I ask dear Mrs. Allan if I can be excused Monday and Tuesday of next week with that time deducted from what I've accumulated. She tells me that it most certainly can be arranged. When I receive a letter from Paul telling me he'll be in my area this coming Friday and asks if he can see me, this time I *want* a day off. But why did it have to happen at the last minute before my trip with Gloria? I'm annoyed, and at first I feel like it's Paul's fault until I realize something must have come up at the last minute. Shame on me for judging when I know none of the facts. Will Mrs. Allan grant me these additional hours? When I meet with her, I sense from my apologies that she understands and says in her gracious manner that she's happy to deduct those hours as well. "You've earned it, Jenny," she assures me. "The time belongs to you."

Paul requested that I be ready to leave at eight o'clock Friday morning when he'll pick me up at the mansion. As usual, he's on time because when I open the manor's front door I see him driving up to the building. Mrs. Allan was delighted when I agreed to be back by nine o'clock to get Shirley ready for bed. Of course, that includes reading or telling her a bedtime story which she begs for and truly seems to enjoy. Reading to her daughter is one more simple pleasure I can give Mrs. Allan as she witnesses Shirley's delight. I owe that to her mother because I was the one she trusted over the many applicants who applied for this dream job, and that's exactly what it is.

The day is already showing signs of being a winner. "Spring is such a lovely time of the year," I say to Paul as he drives the car away from the Allan home. "The blossoms are extraordinary, and there's a promise of delicate flowers and warmer days ahead."

He smiles now as he looks at me. "You're so bright-eyed and lovely this morning," he says with a twinkle in his eye. I look away from him and know I'm wearing a black-and–white, polka-dot chiffon blouse and a flowing black skirt that I've had for years. Lovely, he said? I'll believe him because I want to.

"If I'm acceptable, it's due to you," I tell him. "I've really needed this day off, and you make me feel cheerful and as if we are about to have a fun day."

We've been driving for some time along Lake Michigan when he asks, "It's almost time for lunch. What would you say to a picnic? I know where we can get excellent food—Southern fried chicken and all the trimmings—in a town along this highway. How about lemonade to drink, or would you prefer iced tea?"

"Paul, you never cease to amaze me. I suppose you know just where we'll stop the car to enjoy all the goodies? And you know they have picnic tables?"

"I know just the spot above the lakeshore because I checked it on my last trip home. Yes, there are not only picnic tables but swings if you like to go up in a swing, up in the air so blue . . ."

"I think I'll leave that to Robert Louis Stevenson as I prefer keeping my feet on the ground." Our chatter always keeps things light, as it should be.

When we arrive in the picturesque town Paul described, he picks up the food and then drives to the picnic spot he's chosen. I'm not disappointed and see when walking around that we're on high ground that overlooks the shores of Lake Michigan. Paul opens the picnic basket filled with mouthwatering food and removes plates and silverware on which to serve chicken, potato salad, baked beans, rolls, bananas, and cookies. This must be a dream as the food is scrumptious, meeting all my expectations, but as I listen to Paul, I know the company is even better with so many wise comments coming from the man with the golden tongue. Even though I was ordered not to witness the trial, I'm convinced that if another attorney had handled his case Jon would have been sentenced to serve more time than he was given to be locked behind bars. Paul asks about Ruth, and I assure him she arrived safely and that Becky is adjusting to her new life and loves the farm."

How I wish I didn't have to show him the letter I received earlier this week as it might spoil the fun we're having. When we finish eating, I can't delay the ordeal any longer.

"Let's pack up the leftovers, Paul, because there's something I must discuss with you." He looks puzzled as he studies me. We put the remainder of our lunch in the basket and slide the dirty dishes into a separate bag. I look through my purse for Gloria's letter but can't find it although I was sure I had remembered it. I wonder if I left it at the mansion, and if so, I'll have to do my best to let him know what Gloria said in her letter. When I finish, he looks at me with an expression of understanding.

"Without a doubt, this trip will be very difficult for you, Jenny, especially when you don't want Gloria to know anything about the tension between you and Jonathan. Are you sure you can't trust her to know the details?"

"I'm not sure, Paul, but I don't want to chance it. She asked too many questions when I was still in Duluth. If things get bad, I'll have no choice but to tell her about our rift. However, I hope to avoid that. I'll have to handle this the best I can.

"Why did this have to happen?" I'm angry now and stare at Paul as if it's his fault. Pettishly I demand, "Why did that drunken brother of hers have to pay for his bootlegging foolishness and be sent to the same correction facility where my husband is serving time?"

"Life doesn't always give us choices, my dear. Most of the time we have to take it the way it's dished out. Do you think you can break through Jonathan's shell? You told me you haven't seen him since the trial because he continues to ignore you."

"I have no idea how he'll take my suddenly showing up. I only hope I have the strength to go through with this without making Gloria suspicious and opening the door for her to tell my story to those in Duluth. How I'd hate that."

Paul takes my hand in his and continues to hold it as if he can will his own strength into my body and make this trying experience easier.

"I wish there was something I could do to make things easier for you. How do you feel about him now, Jenny? Are you able to forgive him for the way he has neglected you since the trial and also for his affair, which now I'm regretting I ever discussed with you? You shouldn't have that on your mind when you're trying to assess whether it's wise to make a sincere attempt to work out your marriage."

"Oh, Paul, please don't regret you told me. I'm glad you did because something might come up in the future that would truly hurt me if I didn't know what had transpired back then. Don't blame yourself. Right now I have no idea if I even want to try to make this marriage work, and hopefully it will be easier to make that decision after I see Jonathan. There's so much at stake because my children need their father, but what kind of a father will he be after what he's going through? I have no way of knowing what would be best for them. I might try to make this work and yet fail. Then what? But will I forever be sorry if I don't at least try? That is if he even wants to make the effort himself?"

We are both quiet as I'm sure he knows I'm trying to make some sense out of all of this. Then he speaks slowly and with feeling.

"Jenny, this decision is, of course, yours. If you decide you want a divorce, I will help you in any way I can. But if you decide to go back to him, you must do so with putting everything you've got into making a success of it. If it doesn't work, please by all means let me know. I don't want to influence you now in any way, but I feel as if I should at least tell you how I feel even if this isn't the best time. Perhaps it will give you something to think about if all goes wrong."

What on earth is he talking about?

"I'd like us to look back at that night of the Ford/Vincent anniversary party in Laurel Hill. I'd told the Vincents I must leave early as I was in the process of preparing for an important court case due to begin early the next morning. Perhaps it would have been better had I left even sooner.

"You and your husband were seated at the head table with the Vincents. I'd noticed you early on and can still remember what you were wearing—a midnight blue velvet dress with a beige collar and cuffs of some type of soft, flowing material, the very dress you wore the night of our first visit to Rudolphs. Believe me when I say that I never thought much about what women wore before that night. I was much too engrossed in my work to even notice the opposite sex. I dated seldom because the occasions were always a disappointment, and I considered them a waste of time. The mystery was 'why did I notice you, Jenny?'

"That evening, I started for the head table to say good night to the Vincents but backed off when I saw Governor Lanesboro, who had been invited by the Fords, approach you. I couldn't help but overhear his words as he leaned toward you. 'May I have this dance with the loveliest woman here?'"

"Oh my gosh, Paul, that's exactly what he said. I knew I wasn't the loveliest woman at the party, but there must have been something about my happiness that night that made me look special—or the loveliness of the dress I wore. I can hardly believe you remember the words."

"Oh yes, I will never forget them. But the day I was introduced to you outside the courtroom made such an impact on me that it's haunted me ever since. Your eyes were not sparkling with excitement as they were that evening in Laurel Hill. They were pitifully sorrowful on the day of that trial. After it was over, I kept wondering what harm there could be in asking to see you again to determine why you hadn't gone into the courtroom to listen to the proceedings. Didn't you want to know if your husband would be sentenced, or didn't you care? I didn't have to see you to learn the reason, but I *wanted* to know. Why had Jonathan strayed from the home fires. Didn't he love you, but how could he not?"

"Oh, Paul, how can I help you understand when I don't even know myself?"

He takes my hand as he says, "If things don't work out, my dear, please let me know. I'm not sure but perhaps I've told you too much already. I want you to think clearly about whether or not you believe you can mend your marriage. At this time I cannot be a part of this. But if you *really try* and it doesn't work out, I hope you will allow me to be first in line to pursue the loveliest lady in our picnic area."

I smile at him and nod my head *yes* as he takes my hand again and says, "May I interest you in a walk, my lady?" I saw a path that leads down to the lakeshore. Let's take our things to the car before we head for the sandy beach."

We stroll hand in hand at first, attempting to shake away, best we can, the serious talk we've just had. I take off my slippers and walk barefoot so I can feel the sand sifting through my toes. It's a warm feeling, and I find peace for some time. We speak little, and I'm sure he knows I need time to let all this serious discussion penetrate my confused mind.

Eventually we resume our chatter. We joke, then laugh, and again totally enjoy each other. When we turn around to return to the path that leads to the car, Paul says he noticed the movie *Flying Down to Rio* is playing in the small town where he bought the food. "Would you like to see it? I hear there's a new dance team playing in it—Ginger Rogers and Fred Astaire."

"That would be fun," I tell him as we head for the car.

As we near the city on our return, we see a small tourist area where we're attracted to a gorgeous sight over Lake Michigan—a cloud-filled sky and a dipping sun about to submerge behind trees. "Shall we stop and watch this bewitching scene?" Paul asks. We sit quietly in the car as, with hands locked, we drink in nature's beauty.

Apparently the beauty moves him as much as it does me because his arm comes compassionately around me as he holds me as close as possible in these cramped quarters. Our lips touch softly at first, then more tenderly, and finally more passionately than I've ever experienced. Never have I been more moved and felt such intense yearning. To break away now is so difficult that it takes all my strength.

When I'm far enough away so it's safe, I say, "I know I'm committed to making this marriage work, Paul, but be assured that if you still want me, and I feel the way I do now, you most definitely will be the first in line if the marriage fails."

When I return to the Allan home and tuck Shirley in bed, I'm happy to retire early because I need the rest. My mind, however, is unable to stop whirling.

I review the day and know that whatever Paul and I do together we enjoy. He's a superb companion and friend. We came out of the theater singing the songs from the movie and laughing joyfully as we rehashed the scenes. How difficult it was to say good night. We both know what lies ahead. It's probably good that I begin experiencing the rugged road I must tread. A job never gets done by merely thinking about it.

Difficult as it is to pack and get ready to leave with Gloria Monday morning, I know I must. It's not that I don't want to see my friend; it's only that it will be extremely difficult to meet with Jonathan. For that matter, I'm not sure he'll even agree to see me. I haven't had time to tell him I'm coming.

Chapter 23

A Visit to Jonathan

Jenny

Gloria, my friend of many years, finds the Allan home with no problem. I must give her credit for her ability to know how to drive and read maps. Those are skills I've never acquired—certainly not with a husband who had no patience with me. Jonathan would lose his temper if I'd make but a tiny error, and that would cause me to be so nervous I couldn't think clearly and would make constant mistakes.

I remind Mrs. Allan that I plan to return Tuesday evening. What a blessing that she asks no questions as to where Gloria and I are headed.

I make an effort to remain calm but am paralyzed with fear. As we begin our trip, Gloria chatters for approximately fifteen minutes though I hear little of what she's rambling on about and only nod my head in agreement whenever she pauses.

Whatever will I say to Jon? Will he be as bitter as he was when I last saw him? Will he be excited about his release in August? I must be on my guard not to slip and inform him I know about that timing as he might wonder who told me. I don't want to betray Paul.

"You're so quiet, Jenny," Gloria says. "When did you last visit Jon?" Her comment makes me realize I'd better join in the conversation as we two haven't seen each other in some time. She might grow suspicious of my rocky relationship with my husband. That's confirmed when she repeats her last question.

"Maybe you didn't hear me. When did you last visit Jon?"

"I'm not sure," I tell her without skipping a beat. I know I've been attempting to avoid telling her too much. To sound more pragmatic I add, "I have to be very careful with my money because I try to send something on a regular basis to the people who are caring for our children. Hopefully Jonathan will be released before long. Until then, we're just barely managing to get along."

"Then tomorrow will be a very special day for you, won't it?" Gloria asks. "I wish I could say the same about my visit with Gus and his bootlegging shindigs. It's Mother's pressure that pushed me into making this trip. You'd think that bad boy of hers was still a little kid."

I've known Gloria since we were kids and am aware she has never been too fond of her brother Gus. The siblings are so different. Gloria has fought to support herself and earn money the honest way while Gus makes money the easy way no matter who gets hurt. Her harsh words now don't surprise me.

I was given permission by Mrs. Allan to pack sandwiches, and having them makes a lunch stop unnecessary. But we make little of the progress we'd hoped as the roads are narrow and rough. When Gloria suggests stopping for the night and relaxing over a meal, I'm relieved. Although it might mean another night with little sleep, at least this delays my visit to Jon until tomorrow.

We arrive at the Illinois Federal Correctional Facility the next morning and stare in awe at the size of the edifice. It's much larger than we'd expected. Men roam the yards and work in gardens under the watchful eye of guards. My legs once again turn to soft rubber as I'm shown into a stark white room with a table and a few chairs. Thankfully Gus is in another part of the institution, and Gloria isn't present when I see Jonathan for the first time in almost three years.

I know I'm staring at him, but it can't be helped. Jon hasn't changed much although I miss the smart clothes he wore before he had to wear the unattractive prison attire. The customary expression of a confident man is gone, but when he sees that I'm the visitor, life comes into his eyes. It's an eye-opener for me as he's caught me off guard. I'd expected a cold reception.

"This is a surprise," he says with a weak smile. "How did you get here?"

I explain Gus's pranks that have landed him in this institution and tell him Gloria invited me to ride down with her. "Does it bother you to see me?" I ask.

"Of course not. Why should it?"

Now I am puzzled. Wasn't this the man who insisted that I don't enter the courtroom? Wasn't he the one who walked out without so much as a farewell wave to his own wife? I did write him a few letters, but did he answer even one? No. Before I can think of another rejection, he makes an additional comment.

"Okay, okay. So I didn't answer your letters and didn't say good-bye before I was sent here. Do you have any idea how upset I was? Why would you even want to have anything to do with me?"

That's not easy to answer. I ultimately conclude, "After all, you are my husband."

"Yeah, and what a great one I am," he adds. "Are you saying that you could ever let me enter your life again after the foolish mistakes I've made? George must have filled you in on all that garbage."

Rejection would have been easier than this. Forget? Forgive maybe. His piercing coldness was difficult to overlook and caused me to walk a different course. I've learned a great deal about Jon, and it has changed the direction of my life.

"Let's not get into all that," I suggest. "How much longer do you think you'll be here?" I'm grateful that he explains facts I already know so there will be no slipups.

"My lawyer, Paul Baringer, and cousin George have been working on my case since I landed here. I've tried to be a model prisoner and that never hurts. Instead of my sentence of five years, I foresee I'll be released in August. That's less than two years earlier than my sentence of five years." He stares at me no doubt expecting to hear some sign of joy, but my mind delays that. Finally I can register my "surprise" with a smile.

"That's wonderful," I say, knowing it isn't entirely a lie. Silently I assess the timing and see that I can get home to see the children sooner. The more rapidly decisions are made, the better. Oh, Jon, my mind repeats. I tried to understand and know everything could have been so different. Why didn't you treat me like a wife instead of locking me in a cell so much like the one you've been occupying?

We exchange what we know about the children, subjects we can easily discuss without hesitation. What hurts most is that he knows so much more about David and Holly than I do. It's understandable to a point since his sister Alma would share news with him before she'd ever write me. Perhaps she even thought Jon was sending the information to me.

"David had pneumonia?" I inhale sharply. "Why wasn't I told? That's a serious disease that has killed many children, and there's no cure." This truly frightens me. I'm his mother but does Alma believe she is by now? I assess what could have happened. Have I let my children down by leaving them with others? If that's true, I'd better return home as soon as possible.

"When was this? Is he all right?" When he assures me it was some months ago and David is okay, I'm relieved but troubled.

"Unless there's another problem like this, Jonathan, I'd truly appreciate it if you didn't write me at the home where I'm working. I need to keep this job at least a couple months longer. If anyone were to discover you're in a corrections facility, or prison as some might call it, that person could cause trouble for me. People are cruel when it comes to scandal. Regardless, if you're coming home in August, I'd like to be in Duluth a month before you. It might be wise if I plan to arrive there the first part of July."

Finally he agrees to hold off writing to me until I arrive at my mother's home. "I can certainly write you there, can't I?" he asks.

"Of course," I tell him. All this time I hear nothing from him and now he can't wait to write. Life is strange, or is it just *my* life that's weird.

"I've never met Gus, so I hope Gloria meets us somewhere before you leave," says Jonathan. The conversation moves into the healthier arena of Gus and his folly until the man himself makes an appearance.

When Gloria and I leave the facility a short time later, my thoughts are somewhat apprehensive. Now that Jonathan has met Gus, I hope he's learned his lesson and won't try getting into the bootleg business when he returns home. The way he messed with the stock market was bad enough.

Chapter 24

The Unexpected

Jenny

When Gloria drops me off this afternoon, I learn Mrs. Allan left a message that she wants to see me. Our conversation is extremely difficult. Stinging false accusations by two servants, the cook and the second maid, leave me defenseless since I can't reveal the facts. What right have they to accuse me when they don't know the entire story? Mrs. Allan is uncomfortable and struggling to understand, but I appreciate she has the responsibility of maintaining a household and sustaining a reputation. I lose, and the prying and merciless women win.

As my conversation with Mrs. Allan ends, I'm overwrought and want to know more. I race upstairs to see how and where those frightful women obtained their knowledge. I swiftly shuffle through my dresser drawers before I remember that I put Gloria's letter in the larger suitcase that I didn't take with me on my journey to see Jonathan. Kneeling while I open the bag, I discover that some of my belongings have been carelessly tossed about; then I see the envelope of Gloria's letter and find its contents are no longer there. My perception imagines the pleasure erupting on the evil faces of the women as they lose no time sharing the information with our mistress.

No reputable household dares employ the wife of a criminal. I'd kept my secret, but now they had the power to rid the house of what they no doubt consider an undesirable woman. They have never liked me perhaps because I was forming a bond with the mistress and had the most desirable responsibility in the household, that of caring for little Shirley.

When I finish packing, I stand by the window of this charming bedroom and study the spacious lawn and early plantings in the rear of the Allan home. It's late April, and May is the only time the household sees the green grass and tiny leaves bursting with life on the numerous trees. In June, the family and servants move to the lake home for the summer months.

Is this a nightmare or reality? Will this be the last evening that I gaze out this window? How privileged I've been to care for five-year-old Shirley. It's the only position I've relished since moving to Milwaukee. Tomorrow I have no choice but to leave for Duluth.

Mrs. Allan informed her young daughter of my plans to leave, and later when I tuck Shirley in bed, the child clings to me and digs her small fingers into my back as if that had the power to keep her friend from leaving. I brush against her wet cheeks and whisper, "I'll never forget you, dear." I've grown to love the precious child.

It's growing darker. Clouds have covered part of the sun as I observe the remaining portion sink below trees that line the horizon. My mind drifts back to the many enriching lessons I've learned in so short a time. Growing up, I felt cheated that I hadn't been born into a rich family that lived in an expensive home with all the benefits money can buy. During the interval that I've worked in Milwaukee, I've resided as a servant in mansions or handsome homes and learned that money alone doesn't assure happiness.

I've witnessed cruelty beyond anything I've ever encountered or even imagined. In not only one but two experiences, I was powerless to help those being mistreated. I've also known kindness. After I realized how the women gained their knowledge of my past, I related portions of the truth to Mrs. Allan. The understanding woman was sympathetic and paid me for all my accumulated hours plus extra money to help me financially until I find employment in Duluth. She also rewarded me with many of the lovely dresses Shirley had outgrown and expressed hope that they will fit Holly.

My greatest lesson was when I experienced true friendship and perhaps even love. I now know that love should be the sole reason for marrying. A loving home will prepare children for a happier life.

Again I wonder if any harm came to my vulnerable youngsters by being left with relatives to care for their emotional needs during such tender years. Being reunited with my loved ones shouldn't make me uneasy, but now guilt is playing a strong role. At the time I left Duluth, I felt I had no choice. Was I right? Perhaps not, but maybe it was important for me to learn the lessons I absorbed while living in Milwaukee. Life can be complicated.

At first Maggie was the one who concerned me because she's so sensitive. To my surprise, she seems to have adjusted far better than I dreamed she would. I'm no longer haunted by the look of pain in her eyes that I felt when I first left for Milwaukee. The summers Maggie spent at the lake cottage with my mother and Marie's family have been rewarding. She wrote she's made some extraordinary friends.

Now it's David and Holly who are my main concern. Would Alma and Jake try to take David from me if I were to divorce Jon and eventually marry Paul? Their attachment to our son has become so strong that it concerns me. They have no children of their own, and David might have grown too close to them. If my family is unsuccessful in bonding, would they fight me if I wanted to marry Paul? I'm convinced that Holly has been treated kindly, but it was unfortunate she had older people caring for her during such meaningful years. At least she saw her brother David often, and that's more than I can say for Maggie. She seldom had the joy of visiting her siblings.

There's no way I can inform Paul of what's happened, but Mrs. Allan promised to forward any mail addressed to me to Duluth. It's time to move on and face whatever problems might erupt. But I need help. As I realize this, I pick up my

Bible and open it with no particular chapter in mind. My eyes rest on these words:

> *I will lift up mine eyes unto the hills.*
> *From whence cometh my help?*
> *My help cometh from the Lord,*
> *Who made heaven and earth.*

How could any words have been more fitting? Never have I been as desperate as I am now. I need God's guidance because I don't know which path to take. Like my wise mother taught me years ago: "Jenny, when you ask for God's help, you must know that He will guide you to do what's best for you. Maybe you won't like what He says or does, but just remember that He knows the entire picture. When the time is right, your prayers will be answered. Only God knows when that will be or the way it will happen. You must have faith and trust Him."

I get down on my knees by the foot of the bed and ask that God from this day forward will take charge of my life. "Dear Lord, please lead me. I cannot do this alone, but I promise to listen to you and do my best to do your will."

I quietly close the Bible and put myself in God's care.

Chapter 25

Letter from Grace

I've been in Duluth over three weeks and still no word from Paul. Did someone other than Mrs. Allan intercept my mail? That seems unlikely since Paul most certainly would have written again if he didn't hear from me. He knew I was about to make the dreaded trip to see Jonathan, and he'd certainly be anxious to know how that went.

Maybe he's become disinterested or no longer cares. People do change their minds. *Oh, Jenny*, I tell myself, *you know better than that*. If I were ever sure of anything, it's that Paul is my dear friend and cares what happens to me. But what's happened; why this silence? Maybe he believes I want to go back to Jonathan and he should keep his distance. He's had time to think about it, and I haven't been near enough to keep him interested and let him know how I feel.

What's the matter with you, Jenny? Now you're even talking to yourself. Every time I know the mailman is due, I go through this agony until I know if there's some message—any message—from Paul. It's bad manners for a woman to write and ask a man why he hasn't written, but maybe I'll have to do that soon because I can't stand this suspense much longer. I know that Marie is getting suspicious because she realizes more than anyone that I dread writing letters, and until now, I haven't really been interested in the mail. The last few weeks has also given me time to assess my decision.

How does one toss away a jewel, and that's what Paul is. Have I fallen in love?

Get a grip on yourself, Jenny. I pick up a brush and run it through my thick wavy hair. Maybe if I can find a job and am busy all day I won't have time to think about Paul. Not that I'm unhappy to be with my children and family because I am glad to be here, but with this issue unresolved, I'm a wreck. Finding work hasn't been easy either. It seems ages since I filled out applications at a few department stores. Do they believe I'm no longer competent because so much time has passed since I last had a job as a clerk? I know that isn't true, *but do they know?* I can't get work such as I had in Milwaukee because no such jobs are listed in the Duluth paper. I suppose in these bad times that even the wealthy Duluthians are being cautious. Clerking may be my only chance to get work.

Maggie has followed me around ever since I returned; same as she did when I visited at Christmas the year before last. It won't be easy for her when I do find work and am away from home more. That's why I made arrangements for her sister Holly to move in next week. Maggie will be so busy getting reacquainted and caring for her, with Mother's supervision, of course, that it might be a helpful diversion. School is out soon, and Maggie will have many free hours to fill her time with this new project.

It's now three o'clock by my watch. The mail should be here by now. Perhaps today there will be some word from Paul.

Since Mother is visiting a friend from Norway and helping her with some Norwegian baking, tonight Marie and I share household duties. My job is to peel potatoes, but shortly after I begin, I hear my sister scurrying to the door to retrieve the Saturday afternoon mail. My heart beats faster as I hear the front door close.

"Jenny," Marie announces, "here's a letter for you from Laurel Hill." The knife I'd been using to peel potatoes slips, and I yell "ouch" as my heart skips a few beats.

"What happened? Did you hurt yourself?"

"I only cut my finger," I tell her as I watch the blood ooze from it. "Suppose I'd better go upstairs and see if I can find the iodine."

As I pass Marie, I whisk the letter from her hand and head up the stairs. I ache with disappointment as my eyes rest on the return address and see it's not from Paul but from my friend Grace. It had been sent to Milwaukee and then here, so that confirms at least this much of my mail has been sent on. Another long day to wait. Will this never end?

I no longer feel any haste so I toss the letter on the nightstand in my bedroom and dab iodine on my finger. No need to awaken any suspicion. What might happen in the future with Paul is something I can't discuss with anyone; at least, not yet.

It's evening when I'm finally free to read Grace's letter. Maggie is occupied at the kitchen table doing her homework because Marie still insists on an eight o'clock bedtime for her. Although I don't agree that the child should go to bed that early, I'm not about to undermine my sister's training until our family has a home of its own.

I pick up the letter Grace sent and read through the first few paragraphs telling about friends I left behind a few years ago. I chuckle at some of the stories. It isn't until I turn the page and continue reading that I can't believe what Grace is telling me. "Do you remember Paul Baringer?" she writes. Do *I* remember him? I perceive a sudden pride as if he's mine already. Grace continues, "Wasn't he Jonathan's lawyer? From what I understand," she continues, "he had monthly meetings with clients somewhere near Milwaukee or Chicago. On his way home a few weeks ago, he was in a head-on collision. From what the doctor could determine, he died instantly. The whole town has been saddened by the news. We all liked Paul who was a very special person."

Whatever Grace wrote after that was of little importance to me. Did she say he was dead? That can't be true; not my dear Paul. How could life be so cruel as to give me someone so wonderful and then take him away?

My arms hang limply at my side as I have trouble catching my breath, yet no tears fall. The letter drops from my fingers to the floor as I sink into bed like one who is in shock or bewitched. The sky darkens, and I hear raindrops falling outside my window.

I come out of my traumatized state long enough to realize that it's best no one finds me this way or they'll want to know why. Like a dazed corpse, I slip out of my clothes and put on my nightgown. Any moment now, I'll become conscious enough to know I'm only having a shocking nightmare; nothing more.

There are footsteps on the stairs, and I assume it's Maggie. To escape her questions, I lie down and turn on my side. At this moment, I have no answers.

But when I awaken the next morning, I remember nothing of what happened the night before. I rub my eyes yet have this haunting feeling that something is terribly wrong. Did Maggie come to bed and ask, "What's wrong, Mama?"

My head is splitting. Now I remember that the dear child went into the bathroom to get me a cold washcloth. "Here, Mama," she said as she put it on my forehead before climbing into bed to rub my arm gently as if that can work the pain from my body. Then it all comes back and I know it's true. Paul is dead.

Oh, dear God, why? Why did you let this happen? But I know better, so why blame God? He gave man the gift of free will, and we're the ones who make a mess of things. God sees the overall picture while we see nothing but the present pain, and that is so difficult. It hurts bad.

Was it my fault? I upset Paul before he left, didn't I? No, that's wrong. He was the one who reassured me that in all likelihood this would no doubt put the future into motion. I needed to communicate with my husband, but I had no idea it would be the last time I'd see Paul. Now a sob escapes from my throat, and the tears flow like a waterfall.

There's a knock at the door, and it's my sister Marie. She's dressed for work but says she must talk to me first.

"Jenny, what happened? You were fine when you headed upstairs after dinner. Maggie was so upset this morning that she asked that I look in on you.

"I just had a bad night, Marie. I do remember a fierce headache, but it seems to be okay now." I can sense her staring at me.

"But you're not really better, are you, Sis? Whatever it is, don't you think you need to talk to someone? Don't keep this to yourself. You'll go insane."

Maybe I'm crazy already, I tell myself. Paul is gone. My dreams have erupted, and there's nothing left for me.

"What's wrong with me, Marie, reminds me of a song. If I remember the words, it goes like this: 'There's nothing left for me, of things that used to be. I live in memory, among my souvenirs.'"

My voice cracks. My chest heaves until I believe the sadness will choke me. I turn over and put my face into my pillow until I once again gain control.

Marie's voice becomes louder as she insists, "Tell me, Jenny. It does help, you know. Whatever it is I swear to you that I'll never breathe it to another soul—not even Carl. It will be our secret."

An awkward silence follows until I'm finally able to communicate with her.

"It was in that letter . . ."

"What letter?"

But she doesn't know what happened. Since the floodgates have now opened, I begin talking and telling my story. I don't stop until I've stripped my very soul. When I finish, there's silence until Marie comments in a low voice, "Good heavens, Jenny, you've gone through hell these past few years, haven't you? Does Jonathan suspect?"

"No, but his soul isn't pure white either."

She looks surprised. "It isn't?"

My story isn't finished, and I press on to tell what I'd learned about Jon. I knew this was no excuse for what I did, but telling Marie helps momentarily to lift the guilt. Later I realize something has been gained as I no longer am as bitter toward Jonathan. Had he loved this other woman or was it just a lark; another conquest for him?

Does falling in love excuse my actions? Paul was my friend, someone I enjoyed being with. Could I have kept our friendship on but a companionable basis for any length of time? I'd never know now.

"I hate leaving, but I must get to work," Marie says. "I'm already late." She rises slowly and heads for the door.

"Marie?"

She turns to face me.

"Thanks," I say. "You were right as it did help to talk to you about this. I appreciate that you're here for me."

"Isn't that what sisters are for? We might not agree on everything, but how does that saying go? Blood is thicker than water?"

Marie turns to leave but stops.

"Jenny, Maggie was very concerned about you. Do try to get up by the time she gets home from school. Before I leave, I'll tell Mother that you need sleep now to make up for what you failed to get last night."

"I promise I'll be here for Maggie," I tell her. I settle back and close my eyes, but does rest even help?

Chapter 26

Jonathan Returns

Jenny

The skies are still covered with dense clouds from the recent rainfall as I make my way down the sidewalk where the train will stop. The portly engine appears to proclaim its strength as it pulls its overwhelming load toward me. A conductor brushes past me at peek speed, carrying a step stool as he prepares to assist passengers in their descent from the coaches, but I'm so preoccupied with my thoughts that I barely notice him.

What do Jonathan and I have to talk about? This is like meeting a stranger. I only know that I can't allow him to behave toward me the way he has in the past when he's put me down with the crushing power he's always used with me.

What a gift Paul gave me! He made me feel as if I had charisma. I know I'm no beauty, but when I was with him, I felt stunning and as if when I walked into a room, all eyes met mine with admiration. Maybe that wasn't always the case but often I could definitely feel it. Ruth used to tell me I had a certain glow about me when I was with Paul. I gained confidence in myself and felt I could do most anything I put my mind to. I'm stronger because of his caring and know I'm worthy of respect.

The train emits a screeching sound as the brakes bring it to a halt. Passengers slowly appear and are helped to the platform. I stand here for some time before I see Jon. The time has come to put my new attitude and feelings to a test.

Maggie

What's the matter with me? I'm so scared that I'm shaking. Uncle Carl and I sit on an uncomfortable wooden bench while we wait for Mama to find Daddy. He's supposed to arrive on this train, and I wonder if I'll know him when I see him? Will he recognize me? This is taking too long; many people have come off the train but not my Daddy.

Auntie Marie said she wasn't coming with us tonight to meet the train because she has to help Grandma with dinner. I heard Mama say Auntie and Daddy don't get along so good. I thought they did when she and Tommy visited us in Laurel Hill where we had so much fun. Guess I was too little to really notice and remember; or maybe it all changed when we moved to Duluth.

"Here they come, Maggie," Uncle Carl tells me. I feel his eyes on me as I stay seated until he says, "Maybe you should greet your father?"

Why is he making me do that when I'm so embarrassed? This is harder than I thought it would be.

I slowly rise and painfully move toward Daddy. He looks like my daddy and is still tall. I always thought he was handsome, and I guess he still is. His hair seems the same and it's still straight and brown, but isn't he skinnier?

Oh dear. Mama and Daddy seem to be angry about something, so now what's wrong? Mama is so pretty in her pale green dress with a long, straight skirt. She never liked collars and cuffs like Auntie Marie wears. This dress has a big bow drawn to the side of a round neckline, short sleeves, and two large buttons near the waistline. Mama and Daddy would make a handsome couple if they'd just smile once in a while.

That blue suit Daddy is wearing is a nice color and matches his eyes. Didn't he wear that when we lived in Laurel Hill? Hey, I remember the blue striped tie he's wearing.

"Daddy, you're wearing the tie I gave you."

"Oh," he says. "Did you give this to me?"

My mouth opens in disappointment, and then I sigh. He's forgotten. "Daddy, don't you remember? I gave it to you for Christmas."

But he doesn't answer me and talks about something with Mama. Finally he turns to me and says, "How's my girl?" He holds me off and studies me. "I do believe you've grown a little."

Goody. He notices me, and now I'm excited.

"Daddy, do you know what? I used to be the shortest girl in my class, but now there are four girls shorter than me." My words almost flop over one another as I race to tell him. "I'm so happy I'm growing even if I don't fit in my old dresses anymore. Uncle Carl measured me the other day and . . ." I stop talking to inhale and catch my breath and notice Daddy isn't even hearing what I'm saying. He gazes off in the distance and pays no attention.

Uncle Carl leans out the car window and asks me to come up front with him. I do, and Mama and Daddy climb into the back seat.

"Nice car, Carl," Daddy says.

"Thanks."

Silence. Why doesn't somebody say something? It's weird they don't 'cause I always talk to avoid the quiet even though I don't feel like it today. At last, the grown-ups speak a little more, but it's only about dull and dumb things like the weather and cars.

When we near home, I see Holly run out the door, her blond curls bobbing. I'm jealous when Daddy sweeps her into his arms and wonder why he doesn't give me that kind of love. Is there something wrong with me?

Later we sit down to a fine dinner of fried ham with Grandma's special ham-flavored cream gravy to pour over our boiled potatoes, but then it gets quiet again. Again I get nervous so quickly say, "Do you want to go to Grandma's cabin with us this weekend, Daddy?"

“No,” he answers much too loud and fast. “I want to see my mother and sister.”

I hope I didn’t hear him right. Mama has a part-time job clerking in the women’s dress department at Merlin’s Department Store, so now I’m all upset. She only works during the week and has free time every other Saturday. This is the Saturday she has off. If Daddy won’t go to the cabin, will Mama stay in town? Soon school will begin and summer will be over. The worst part is our days at the cabin will be over. I hope I can still spend my summers there.

Everyone goes to bed early, and I’m back in Grandma’s bed. I wake up sometime during the night and hear the muffled sound of voices coming from Mama and Daddy’s room. I think I have to go to the bathroom, so I slip out of bed and put on my slippers before I pause at their closed door.

I hear Daddy say, “No, I didn’t want her to come to the depot. I only wanted *you* there.” He’s talking about me, and big tears well up in my eyes.

“I can’t stay here,” Daddy says. “I’ll talk to Alma in the morning.”

Chapter 27

Living with Alma and Jake

Maggie

The one thing I know for sure is that Aunt Alma is a good cook; it definitely shows by her size. I watch her now as she opens the oven door and shoves in the fat chicken she's stuffed. Aunt Alma has large breasts that jiggle above her huge tummy. When she chuckles, everything on her body moves. Her shoulders are wide, and she has plump arms. I like her little round eyeglasses. They might look funny on some folks, but they fit Auntie's round face.

She also has no teeth. Out of the corner of my eye I watch her "gum" her food. Mama caught me and warned me not to snicker or all my teeth might fall out as punishment for laughing at others. I wiggle my front teeth to make sure they're still okay.

When we're alone I ask Auntie what she meant by gumming her food.

"Well, Maggie, I swish the eats around in my mouth until all is soft enough to swallow. It won't always be this way. When Unkie has a larger plumbing contract, we'll have more money, and then I can buy teeth and a few new clothes."

When we first moved here, Aunt Alma ignored me almost as if I didn't exist. That only made me try even harder to get her to like me. After all, I'm no stranger. I'm Daddy's child, same as David and Holly.

We call Uncle Jake "Unkie." He looks like jolly Saint Nicholas with his twinkling eyes, round belly, and cheerful smile. He loves food and beer. I sometimes wonder how he and Auntie get close enough to hug and kiss when they both have such big bellies.

Everyone loves Unkie. If my aunt and uncle had been rich enough to hire a butler to announce the arrival of guests, it wouldn't be necessary to announce Unkie. He'd walk in, smoking one of his favorite cigars, and the smell would tell you that he was home.

When Unkie grins and laughs, you can't help but feel happy. I love his deep voice when he sings. He has what Mama calls a bass voice that goes way down deep and sounds like one of the trombones we have in music class in school. I could listen to Unkie sing "Old Man River" for hours. I clap like crazy when he finishes to show him how much I love him and appreciate his singing voice.

Jenny

"Alma. What can I do to help?" I ask when I return from running an errand.

"You can set the table if you'd like."

Work was available at Wahl's Department Store during the Christmas season. It went well except I earned far less than I'd hoped. If one had to work overtime, you'd receive no pay for that, but no one complained. We were all just thankful to have a part-time job during the holidays when people spend money they've probably saved for months. Temporary jobs don't come often now until the stores are busy again. With this Depression, who knows when that will be? Those who have steady jobs are barely hanging on.

I'm worried now because with no my extra money coming in, how can we get along? It's humiliating not to contribute to the groceries to show Alma and Jake how grateful we are to them for providing shelter for our family. Jonathan hasn't found steady work so we can rent our own home, and the money I've earned won't last long. I've seen signs in Jon that he doesn't mind taking handouts from his sister and her husband. Has all his pride and responsibility disappeared?

I know he's borrowed money from Mel to buy an old beat-up car for his part-time job of delivering candy and snacks to stores in West Duluth and Hermantown. That's his only temporary job for now. Jon's wages are minimal, and most of the money he's earned has gone to repay Mel for the clunker. Heaven knows what's happened to the rest of what he's earned. I know that wasn't much, but our family sees none of it.

"Will the birthday man be home in time for his party?" I ask Alma who shrugs her shoulders.

"He's supposed to be, but he might run into a problem. The guys he works with are always looking for some excuse to celebrate after work. If they learn it's Unkie's birthday, they'll gather to buy him a glass, or three, of beer. This morning I ordered Jake to keep his birthday a secret so he could be home tonight. I made a bargain with him that he could tell the guys tomorrow and be late coming home then. "Fair enough, don't you think?"

The front door opens, and Maggie rushes to meet Unkie. If it's Jonathan, I know she'll be disappointed.

It is. He's in his usual silly mood as he heads for the table. He picks up a fork in one hand and a table knife in the other and is ready to recite his usual poetry we've all grown weary of hearing.

> Here I sit upon my seat,
> Looking for something good to eat . . .

Noticing that no one was impressed with that, Jon continues with

> I'm a poet
> You don't know it,
> But my feet
> They will show it
> They're Long fellows!

Maggie tries to change the subject. "Mama, I helped Auntie make frosting for the cake. It was fun."

"Good girl, honey. I'm proud of you." We hear the front door open again.

"There's Jake now," Alma says. "I can smell his cigar."

Maggie

Dinner is over, and everyone compliments Aunt Alma on the delicious food. I take special pleasure in the birthday cake since I helped make the frosting. David and Holly are playing the card game "old maid" but naturally didn't ask me to join them. I slide off the uncomfortable chair I've been sitting in too long and wander into the living room to climb into an oversized chair where I can tuck my feet under me to keep them warm. The fire in the fireplace is so burned out it throws no heat. It's not much good anyway as it's so different from the cozy one our family had in Laurel Hill. This whopping big one makes the whole house feel like it's drafty and cold as soon as one leaves the warmth of the fire.

I must be getting used to living here even though it's no fun. It's far from the dream I had when the family was separated. Mama says we had no choice but to move in with Alma and Jake because Daddy wouldn't live with Grandma Nelly and Aunt Marie. He said those Norwegians get on his nerves. When Aunt Alma and Unkie found this house, they said it was big enough for our family to move in with them. Funny how Daddy will live with his but not Mama's sister.

Mama told me we can't afford a home of our own until Daddy gets a steady job. She also said Alma was probably glad to offer some of this house to us so she could keep David with her longer. She spoils Holly too and gives her special treats. Her feeling is that Holly is unhealthy because she's too thin, but she's sure she could fatten her up in no time by giving her heaps of ice cream and some of Unkie's beer. I don't think Mama would like that.

Something else puzzles me. When I first went to live with Grandma Nelly, Aunt Marie, and Uncle Carl, I was miserable and lonesome and could hardly wait for my family to get back together. Now I feel I've lost those I left behind when we moved here. Now I miss quiet times with Grandma

Nelly when we'd play 500 Rummy or she'd teach me cooking secrets or how to embroider. She told me about her past too when she had very hard times after her Mama died. She had to move in with her Grandma who was real mean to her.

Uncle Carl was nice and at times helped me with my homework. We'd discuss things in the newspaper like when someone kidnapped Lindbergh's baby son. I felt really sad and don't think I'll ever forget that.

I even got used to that little pest Tommy and played tinker toys with him when he'd let me. We had our most fun romping with Ted Bear, our little kitty that we both loved. I miss Ted Bear too, more than I can say. Auntie Alma said we could get a kitten for this house but no cat could be a substitute for Ted Bear. I was surprised how much I missed my "other family" and can't understand any of this.

Because I live in a new area now, I had to change schools. I hate that big, tall school I attend now with none of my old friends in my class. One bright moment was when the mother of one of the boys brought ice cream bars to us at school to celebrate his birthday. Boy, was that swell. I found out later that his folks own a grocery store, so they must be rich and could afford it.

Christmas was sad because I had no money to buy presents. There wasn't much in gifts for me except some warm mittens Grandma Nelly knitted. Our stockings held only an apple, an orange, and a few pieces of hard candy. I only like soft chocolates like we get a few of at the Sunday school program. Maybe Santa is poor like the rest of us.

Daddy is the one who is certainly different than he used to be. He's mean to me, and once gave me a spanking in front of the neighbors for something I didn't even do. He's so crabby with Mama and hardly stays home nights but goes out with that icky Mel. Mama says they go bowling, and we have no money for that. I'm not the only one who's mixed up.

Jenny

I don't know how much longer I can stand this. I was so devastated when I learned Paul died. Without him, how will I ever escape from Jon? If Paul had lived and I tried to get a divorce, I'm positive now that Jonathan would have made my life miserable. I'm also convinced he's lied about me. He's said many hateful things already and probably told falsehoods to his mother. She doesn't like me and seldom talks to me except with a nasty tone in her voice. What have I done to hurt her?

Jon spends money he shouldn't squander and doesn't seem to care if Alma is given grocery money or if our children have necessary clothing. I never knew him to be so selfish. He used to take pride in caring for us but now says he missed out on a lot of his life while at the correction facility and is determined to make up for it now. He wasn't the only one who missed what we could have had as a family.

Alma and Jake are going to visit relatives tonight and take them some birthday cake. Will Jon and I have time to communicate then?

Maggie

Mama bathed David and Holly and put them to bed, so now it's my turn. I scrub myself real good. When I'm through, I step out of the tub to rub myself with the towel. Then I hear angry voices coming from downstairs. At first, I can't understand the words until they get so loud that I just know Mama and Daddy are fighting again. This sounds worse than ever before.

I pull the plug to drain the water and yank on my robe and slippers. Then I realize if I sneak to the top of the stairs I can hear better. I can always wipe out the tub later.

Mama talks louder now. "I like Alma, but she always tries to reverse every suggestion I give David. You'd think she was his mother instead of me."

"And what do you propose I do about that?"

"For starters, you could support me a little," Mama says. "It's not easy living with others when I'm always overruled when it comes to my children. We need a place of our own, Jonathan. You could try harder to find steady employment so we could get out of here."

"Damn it, Jenny. You don't know what it's like. Just like when I applied at the bank and they told me they couldn't hire me because of my record. I knew what they meant. No one wants to hire someone who has served time especially in these rough times. I can't even stand the strain of filling out applications anymore."

"You mean you're not even trying?"

It gets so quiet it scares me. I don't hear Daddy answer. After a while I hear Mama say, "The children need shoes. If you aren't even trying to find something that pays more than this delivery job, you could cut back on your nights out with Mel. He should be spending his time with someone who has no responsibilities and can spend money however he pleases rather than going out with a man who has a wife and three children to support."

I shiver as I listen. I hate it when they fight.

"Now you're telling me who I should see and how to spend my money?" Daddy yells. "I can see anyone I choose and whenever I care to."

"You've changed," Mama says. "You used to spend time with me. Now it's as if the children and I don't exist. Don't you care about us anymore?"

Daddy speaks very slowly. "Maybe it's just *you* I can't stand. You're always complaining. I guess I'd better find a little shack in the woods to live in."

I see Mama coming around the corner. I shrink back so I can't be seen. She sounds even madder at Daddy. "Why don't you just do that. Find yourself a little shack in the woods. Every conversation we ever have ends with those words."

I peek out again and see Mama turn and dash for the stairs as she calls, "You're always threatening to run off somewhere."

But Daddy follows and shouts so loud I feel like covering my ears. "Now who's running?" he shouts. "Come back here," he says as he grabs her arm.

"Let go of me! You're hurting me."

Daddy pulls her, so she starts to lose her balance and almost falls. Her body is now turned toward him, and he slaps her face so hard I can hear the smack. Again he raises his hand to hit her as she grabs the railing.

"Stop it!" I sob as I race down the stairs as if I'd been shoved from above.

"Don't you hit my Mama," I shriek as I pound his chest with all my strength.

"That's right," he whines as he grabs my wrist. Mama's little girl. You're quite a spitfire, aren't you? You be sure to save your Mama from your nasty Daddy."

He turns and walks down the stairs to grab his coat from the coat rack by the door. I watch him go out and see him slam the front door so hard it shakes.

Holly and David stand by their doors, whimpering. Mama rushes to them to take them in her arms to coax them back to bed. 'Mama's little girl' keeps playing over and over in my head.

After some time, Mama comes to me. "Maggie, dear, I think it's time you stopped calling me mama." That isn't what I thought she'd say.

"What should I call you?"

"How about Mother?"

"Oh, Mama. That's what old people say."

"Well, then, how about Mom?"

I consider that. "Guess it's okay, but I like Mommy better." Maybe she's right. It's time to change that word. I crawl into bed but am still quivering when she enters and tucks me in.

Sleep won't come. About an hour later, I hear the front door quietly open and shut. There are no voices, so it must be him. I don't know if I'm glad or sad that he's back.

Chapter 28

The Secret

Jenny

"Jenny, what have you done?"

What was that? I glance around the dark room. Am I hearing things? I retired as soon as I was sure the children were asleep, but I can't settle down. All I do is toss and turn, and now I'm hearing voices?

"Go away," I order as I place my hands over my ears.

"I can't, Jenny, not until you think this situation through and know what you must do to pull this family together."

I can't think anymore tonight. The voice becomes totally quiet. I don't like that either, but I know I should listen. *Could that be my own voice?*

I'm quiet and then resume trying to make sense out of what's happened. It's back again.

"I've never known you to argue, lose your temper, and shout especially when your dear children are within hearing range. That isn't you, Jenny."

Unhappiness has been tearing me apart lately, and I keep thinking of what might have been. I've almost forgotten how much I longed to be with my children, which means I must get along with my husband as well. Could it be that I just don't understand him?

There—you've got it! You're feeling sorry for yourself. What you're going through isn't easy, I'll give you that, but you're blowing it, Jenny. Start thinking about *why* your husband acts this way and what will make the situation easier.

When I finish getting those thoughts together, I no longer hear the voice. Where did you go? But there's no one here. You're talking to yourself, you idiot.

The rest is up to you, Jenny. Be ready when he returns.

Be ready? You're back again? Now what are you asking of me? I'm supposed to begin thinking about why Jon is acting this way? Right now I don't want to think about him at all.

Concentrate, Jenny, so that by the time he gets here, you're able to grasp why he's acting this way. It can't be that difficult.

Fifteen minutes later, I hear the front door open and close. That must be him. It's time.

He says nothing when he enters the bedroom, and I lie very still. He removes his clothes and slowly slides into bed. It's silent for a moment, and then he turns toward me and takes my hand. That's my signal. I hold his grasp tighter, and so it begins. One attempt at a time.

Maggie

A month has passed since that terrible fight that's been pounded into my memory, and Daddy has been a little nicer to me. I've just returned from the church across the street where the minister spoke in English instead of the Swedish that I can't understand. The sermon was about honoring your father and mother. That troubled me, and I must talk to Mom about it. I find her in the kitchen and tell her I've got a problem and need to talk. She suggests a walk.

A warm May day greets us as we open the door. I fill my lungs with the fresh, balmy air. I suggest to Mom we go to the park that's a mile away. Walking is always fun because it reminds me of cabin days and the frequent hikes Joanna and I took to the small town of Bailey.

Mom points to buds on the lilac bushes. "It won't be long before they'll be in full bloom," she guesses as we pass many houses in the area.

"Now, Maggie, tell me what's bothering you."

"It's just that the pastor said we should memorize what it says in Exodus 20:12. It says, 'Honor thy father and thy mother that thy days may be long in the land which Jehovah thy God giveth thee.'"

"My goodness, but I'm proud of you, honey, for memorizing that. But what don't you understand?"

"Mom, if that's true, I won't live very long."

We've reached the park and are approaching a bench. I look up at the buds that are about to burst on the branches of the trees. Mom takes a handkerchief out of her pocket and wipes the bench seat so we won't get our clothes dirty.

After we're seated, I tell her, "I understand the part about honoring my mother, but it makes me upset when I think God expects me to honor my father."

"You're still angry, aren't you, dear?" Mom asks. I can tell she's studying me, and that makes me squirm.

"It wasn't just that terrible night. Since Daddy came back to Duluth, he hasn't been like the father I remember. He spanked me in front of the neighbors when I wasn't even guilty, and he seems to like only David and Holly. He ignores me except to tell me I remind him of your relatives. I don't think he means that as something nice, does he?" I look up at her and wait for an answer.

She smiles. "Perhaps not, Maggie, but if you're angry with Daddy for that burst of anger last month, you'd better be irritated with me as well. I, too, was guilty."

Troubled, I stare at her. "What do you mean when you say that you're guilty?"

"I'm sure you know it hasn't been easy for me living in someone else's home. David lived with Aunt Alma long enough to make him feel like she's his mother. She takes over, and it's difficult to keep my mouth shut. I need to be in control of your brother before he's completely spoiled. It isn't my house so that would cause problems.

"So you see, it wasn't only Daddy who was upset that night. I was also guilty. We talked too much, too fast, about impossible changes that caused the anger between us to build. The result was we both lost control. Alma and Jack had gone out for the evening, so we knew we had privacy. I was so emotional that I forgot about you children who were within hearing range. Making an endeavor to stop the arguing, I ran off, but unfortunately Daddy followed me. You know the rest. It's true he shouldn't have hit me, but I don't think he'll ever try that again. I believe the real key is understanding."

"Understanding?" I ask. "Understanding what?"

"The time has come to tell you some things about your Daddy. I was going to wait until you were older to tell you this, but I now see that you will have to know at this time in order to understand. But your brother and sister are still too young, so for now this must be our secret. It's Daddy's decision if he wants to tell David and Holly when they grow older."

Mom tells me the true reason we left Laurel Hill, why he was sent to the correction facility, the real reason she left for Milwaukee, and the honest-to-goodness explanation for Daddy finding it difficult to locate work.

"My daddy was in a correction facility? Is that like a jail or maybe a prison?"

"They have a little more freedom, dear, but it's still a prison. The man who reported to Daddy and stole the money from the bank where they worked invested a great deal of money in the stock market. I should make that simpler for you to understand. Daddy was his boss. What is sad is that Daddy knew what crime Art was planning to commit but for some reason didn't try to stop him. Right now I don't have an answer for that. When the stock market crashed and Art couldn't replace the stolen money, he was sentenced to time in prison. Daddy's crime was bad but the lesser one, so he fortunately was sent to a federal correction facility where men are allowed the freedom to work at assigned tasks under supervision.

"Don't misunderstand me, honey. Daddy paid a terrible price for the wrong he did. He lost his dignity and respect. Now people don't want to hire him because he served time. That isn't easy for him. These are hard times with little work available, and I know it hurts him to hear from me about the needs of you children when he can't provide for you. He used to drive the latest model cars and has been reduced to driving an old rattletrap. His pride drags on the ground behind the car."

"You say funny things, Mom."

"I didn't mean to be funny because I've learned something about pride these past few years. I'm not sure if it's good or bad when you lose your pride. Maybe having not too much and not too little is the best after all.

"As for you, my dear daughter, God says you must honor your father and mother if you want to find favor with Him. No matter what Daddy did or does, he's still your father. I know he was wrong when he provoked you to anger, but that's his problem. The Bible isn't easy to understand, but when you're thirteen years old and study for confirmation, it will help you to sort things out."

Maggie

Oh boy, now I have more to think about. I'll do my best to figure out why Daddy acts the way he does so I can do what God and Mom expect of me.

I shrug my shoulders as we approach Auntie and Unkie's home. Life has so many lessons to learn that it shakes me up like a malted milk.

Chapter 29

A Week to Remember

Maggie

It's good that no one can see me now 'cause I'm sitting here pouting. Summer for the last few years has been going to the cabin and having fun with my friend Joanna and her family. During the school year, I used to enjoy the company of my winter friend Elaine. Last summer, she went with us to the cabin so she could see the place I love and meet my friend Joanna. We now live with Aunt Alma and Unkie, and I never see Elaine anymore because I live in a different school district and attend Bell Tower Elementary that sits way up on the hill. I'm in the fifth grade, and all my friends from before are still going to the school that's across from Grandma Nelly's house.

The reason Mom says I can't go to the cabin this summer is that we must stay together as a family, and I should spend time with David and Holly. The kids don't like me and refuse to involve me in their activities, nor are they interested in what I enjoy, so what's the use? What will Joanna and her family think—that I don't care about them anymore? Will they miss me? I'm just miserable and don't know what to do with myself.

I could walk because it's always been fun, but where's the joy in walking alone? Joanna and I used to walk to Bailey many times during the summer. That's three miles there and three miles back to the lake to go swimming, which was really fun. I can't do that here in the city.

After Christmas Mom and I took walks after supper, and that was a good time. We'd put on warm clothing and shuffle through the packed snow with some fluffy stuff still falling. One of those special walks was after Christmas when we passed a row of houses where folks hadn't pulled their shades. From the sidewalk, we'd sneak a peek into their living rooms and see Christmas trees decorated with tons of colored lights. Sparkling tinsel hung in long strips to dangle from every branch. Those special times are glued solid into my brain, so I'll never forget them. On the way home, we'd pass streetlights near the corners where the snow glistened like diamonds. Oh, the glory of it all.

But those walks didn't last long when she felt she must help Aunt Alma.

Now it's spring again, and I'm looking forward to a boring summer. Then on the last day of school, Mom comes to meet and surprise me with wonderful news so great I feel like it is being served on a silver platter. She said Aunt Marie is taking some vacation to spend a week at the cottage and has invited Mom and me to join her family and Grandma Nelly for the week. Daddy, Holly, and David can come on Saturday and Sunday. I hurry to pack my clothes even though I know it won't happen for almost a week, and I can barely keep from jumping up and down. I thank God for this gift that I wasn't smart enough to ask for but that He gave me anyway. The time passes so slowly that I'd like to give the days on the calendar a shove.

On the day we are to leave and Uncle Carl's car finally pulls up to the house, I can tell the kids are jealous but nothing stops us because Mom has been feeling so weak lately that Auntie Marie says she needs a vacation. The doctor told Mom she has stomach ulcers, and since he's the boss, he lays down the law and says she must take the medicine he prescribes.

When we arrive at the lake, my first thought is to find Joanna. I do just that and leap up the hill to their back screen door to yell, "Surprise!"

Jenny

Even carrying the small suitcase and a few groceries to the cabin wears me out. I've really been downhearted lately, and it'll be good to have a change of scenery. Maybe I can somehow put a halt to this depressed feeling I have.

"What a beautiful day," Marie says as she and Carl open the window of the cabin and let in the fresh country air. Nelly is getting a fire going in the stove so she can make coffee while Carl tends to seeing that we have enough water to last a few days. I'm happy Marie has Tommy with her. Those two need to spend time together, and hopefully this will be a happy week for everyone.

After supper and we've said good-bye to Carl until Friday evening, Marie asks Mother if she'll put Tommy to bed so we two sisters can have time to visit. We also need a short walk to take the kinks out. I check on Maggie and see that she and Joanna are sitting on the lot next door waiting for the sun to set. No need to be concerned about them.

As we begin our uphill stroll, Marie says, "Sis, you were doing okay in getting back on your feet after the tragedy, but now I've noticed a change in you. What's eating you?"

Am I that transparent? I should get this off my mind, but would Marie be as understanding as she was after my last crisis? I would have no problem talking to Ruth because I knew it would go no further, but can I trust Marie? What was it she said, "That's what sisters are for." Should I give her a chance? She's right that I do need someone to talk to.

"You must be sure to keep this to yourself, Marie," I instruct her. "If anyone finds out, it would cause no end of trouble."

"Jenny, for Pete's sake, trust me, and you will see that I mean you no harm and certainly won't gossip."

I suppose she's right. "Naturally it's about Jonathan," I say. "Our financial situation was bad enough when he used his small wages to pay Mel the money he'd advanced so Jon could buy the car. Now that's paid for, but the two of them spend money bowling at least two nights a week, and that money should either go to Alma and Jake for food or buy clothes for the children who need shoes for school most of all as they're growing out of them. Even taking them to a shoemaker to patch won't help. We've had a serious fight over this that involved Maggie, and it made me ill to think about it. Heaven knows what Jon and Mel will do next. At least I hope they stay in town and don't cross the river into Superior where there's so much temptation."

"You mean the cathouses?" Marie adds.

"Shhhh." I tell her. "Voices carry."

"Oh, Jenny, I know what a financial catastrophe is. My salary isn't stretching, and Carl can't find anything but odd jobs. I hope the government creates more work soon. President Roosevelt said the CCC will be the next opportunity, and Carl is particularly excited about reforestation that's included in that package. But it isn't happening fast enough, Jenny. Right now I'm the main breadwinner, and if things don't get better soon, I won't be able to continue paying the mortgage on Mother's house, and we could lose it."

After hearing that unwelcome news, my own problems shrink. Lose Mother's house? Why, it's been in the family for years. Not only would losing the property be tragic but where would Mother live? I have no place for any of them as we have no home of our own. I doubt Dad can help as he hasn't sent money in some time.

"I have a suggestion," Marie says. "We have no answers at this time so why not bury our problems for the week we're here and not think about them. We *can* do it, you know. What we should do is thank God for what we have and ask his help in using our wild imaginations to believe we're financially solvent. We have to breathe deeply and relax the best we can so we're more rested and able to think clearly to find what possibilities lie in the future."

I sense my mouth slowly opening as I listen to how she's putting this plan together. "Marie," I tell her, "that's the best idea you've had in years."

The week is unforgettable. We walk, catch and eat crappies, sunfish, and pike; not to mention swim, play cards, and enjoy our children. Not once does it rain. Joanna's brothers and sisters spend time on the beach with Maggie and Tommy. We laugh ourselves silly over the youngest Kelly who's also named

Maggie. We rename her "Little Maggie" so everyone doesn't get confused as to which Maggie folks are addressing. She has such cute ways and delights us. Only five years old, little Maggie is encouraged to stay close to the shoreline. We sit on the hill under the big pine tree when Marie remarks about how long the coarse hair on Little Maggie's legs is growing. I nudge her to remind my sister that sound carries with abundant power over water. Did Little Maggie hear us? I certainly hope not, but if she did, somehow it doesn't seem to have bothered her. Soon she looks up to where we are sitting under the immense pine tree and shouts as she slowly drags her monotone voice, "That's nothin'. You should see all the hair on my Pa's belly." Marie and I double over with laughter.

Jonathan comes to the lake on Saturday with David and Holly, and cousin George comes later to take movies. Everyone gets along better than I can ever remember. Swimming is scheduled for the afternoon where there is no end to joy. After a delicious pike supper, the men build a bonfire on the beach, and we all roast marshmallows to put on graham crackers and blocks of Hershey bars. Delicious! We sing songs, too, but no one has a good singing voice like Unkie. We need him. Thorngren's dog Shep arrives with the Thorngren children, and there is no end to petting the beautiful and kind animal. Jonathan brought firecrackers that we all enjoy; after which the children are given a sparkler to hold while he lights each one. Sparks flash in every direction, and of course, David makes a large circle with his to make everyone ooohh and ahhhhh.

This is a lovely place that we're truly fortunate to have. Maggie told us later that she told the kids in school about Grandma Nelly's cabin to which they responded that not one of them is so lucky as to have a grandparent who owns a cabin by a lake. Now I understand why Maggie enjoys it so much here, and hopefully arrangements can be made for her to have an occasional visit. Marie and I share how grateful we are that we put our can of worms to rest for at least a week. We're now better equipped to handle our problems.

Chapter 30

An Unexpected Turn of Events

Jenny

After our recent fierce argument, Jonathan has been much kinder to Maggie and to me. His efforts make me supportive and more respectful.

It's a cool summer day, and I've accomplished significant tasks around the house helping Alma and Jake. I'm on my last responsibility—that of washing and drying the noon dishes. I hope to accomplish this task before they return from grocery shopping.

Is that them now? "Hello," I call out. But it's Jonathan whom I hadn't expected until this evening. What he says makes me drop my towel on the floor.

"Jenny, good news. I've just been offered a steady job." My knees feel as if they're going to buckle, so I pull out a chair and sit at the kitchen table. I speak hesitantly as if I'm afraid he'll give me the wrong answer. "You did accept, didn't you?"

"Of course. I'm not insane."

"Oh, Jonathan, that's wonderful! I'm so thrilled. But tell me more."

"I'm being employed by the St. Louis County Welfare Department, and their office is in downtown Duluth. The salary isn't bad for a beginner. I'll get $75 a month plus a car allowance, and that should take care of gas and oil plus a car. I'll need something better to drive than the old clunker I'm using now as there will be considerable travel on country roads."

"I definitely agree," I tell him.

"My duties are to stop at addresses the office gives me and interview people on welfare. Without counting the car allowance, we have $75 a month to live on."

"If I understand this, you'll be writing reports on each home you visit?"

"Yup. There are mainly farms but some single homes. Loans have been made to farmers so the families won't lose their investments, and my job is to see that the money is paid back to the county and on time. If not, I'm to ask why not?"

I rise and walk over to him. With my arms around him in a tight embrace, I tell him how happy I am for all of us. "That's such good news that I feel like you've just laid a huge bouquet of roses at my feet."

"Let's not get carried away," he says.

Perhaps I am, but why not since all that matters now is that we're able to gather our flock and live as a family.

"What would our limit be for renting a house?"

Jon takes out pencil and a notebook and jots down some figures. "It should be no more than $20 a month. How soon do you want to start looking?"

"Let's not tell anyone about this until we find a house. Is tomorrow too soon to begin our search?"

Jonathan rises early and leaves to find a phone to call the rental agency and make inquiries. He also buys a newspaper to leave in the front seat while he finds Alma and makes some excuse as to where we're going. She agrees to watch the children, and Jon explains we don't know how long it will take. With that accomplished, we begin the journey into our future.

The first three houses we see meet our price, but they are disappointing because they're old, dark, and gloomy. I'm beginning to get discouraged as I realize $20 a month doesn't seem like much money to rent a house. When we near the fourth house in West Duluth, we aren't too sure this will be any better. An attractive woman opens the door and is wiping her hands on her apron as she greets us. "I'm Joan Tyler," she says. When we tell her we're interested in renting the house, she shakes her head and says she's not the owner.

"My husband and I have been renting this house for two years, but we're moving out of town next week. I don't have a phone so I can't call the Richardson's, but I've offered to show the house. The owners live a few blocks south of here, so if the place meets your needs and they find you are acceptable renters, you'll have to work out the business end of it with them."

We first walk into a small enclosed front hall where coats are hung on one side. Next we enter the living room through a glass French door. My heart skips a beat as I view the bright room with its three front windows facing a modest porch and front yard. On the wall to the left, there's an oblong window high above the floor. We could put our piano along this wall. Jon used to play this instrument with gusto not even needing music as he played by ear. He's barely touched the ivories since returning home, but now there's hope.

The dining room is another joy with two windows that look out over a vacant lot next to us. The sunlight streams through the glass to make the room glow. Our buffet can be placed under another high oblong window on the next wall. Perfect!

The kitchen isn't exactly the room I've dreamed of, but it's passable. A table could be put under the two windows that face the side of a house. I don't like the ugly gas stove, but maybe someday we can buy one. There's no refrigerator; only an icebox. But I like the sizable pantry on the south side that's next to the door that opens to a small back porch. Steps lead off it to a wooden sidewalk that continues around this side of the house.

"The garage is in the basement," Mrs. Tyler says, "but the advantage is that the car is always warm in the winter as the basement is heated by the furnace."

Another plus is that the house overlooks Western High School where the children can walk a couple blocks to attend when they reach that grade level.

The stairway to the second floor is at the far end of the living room. We climb the steps, and when we reach the top we find three bedrooms, a bath, and a generous hallway where there's a cove and I can set up my sewing machine. Off the back bedroom, we note there's a door to the left of the double windows where we find a flat deck with guard rail and where one can place chairs to enjoy a hot summer night's breeze off Lake Superior. There's also an area to shake rugs or a dust mop.

Jon asks Mrs. Tyler how much rent the owners are asking, and we're told $25 a month. My hope falls like a brick being dropped from a high building. Jon will never agree to that because it would take a third of our monthly salary. She tells us that the owners purchased this home as an investment, so she doubted they'd drop the price. If anything, the price might even climb.

After a pause my husband says, "Well, my wife is fussy about where we live, so I guess $25 would be agreeable with us. I'll talk to the owners today."

"If you wish to go with me to the lower level," Mrs. Tyler invites, "you'll note the garage is on one side, a coal bin and furnace nearby, and laundry tubs at the bottom of the stairs." All this makes me quiver as I have a picture of washing and hanging clothes in the basement during the cold weather months. Where will I hang them to dry? This area isn't the most pleasant, but it isn't everything. I've fallen in love with the majority of the house.

We discover when walking outside that there's a huge lilac bush beginning to flower in the back yard plus several currant and gooseberry bushes on one side of the house. A small garden could be put in to extend from the lilac bush to the alley. That will help save on grocery expense. I can make currant jelly from various bushes on the property, plus gooseberries to make great sauce. If I can vegetables from the garden to fill the many shelves I noticed in the basement, that will also save money.

Gorgeous hollyhocks are growing on one side of the house. Soon we'll see the tops of them from the dining room windows.

There's a garden plot near the front porch that Maggie will enjoy for planting her favorite flowers.

“I’ll give you the address of the owners,” Mrs. Tyler says. “They live three blocks south, and we always walk to their home to pay the rent. It’s a pleasant stroll and saves a stamp.” She shakes our hands. “I can tell that you like the place, so good luck.”

We thank her for her kindness and drive to the Richardson home. I say a silent prayer of thanks to God when we make arrangements to rent the house from the owners. As we walk out of their home, Jon says, “Then I guess it’s time to start packing. I begin work Monday, so there isn’t much time.”

I’m having difficulty sleeping tonight. I keep going over the moment I first heard the good news that John has a steady job meaning we can finally have our family together in our own home. Then I try to remember every room in the house we’ve rented. What a joy it will be to live together under one roof without inconveniencing our kind relatives no matter how helpful they are.

I was sure the children would be excited, but Maggie’s joy was overwhelming and greater than I could have imagined. When I told her we’d be living only a few blocks from her former school where she could enroll in the sixth grade, she was ecstatic. David and Holly could attend this school too.

So much joy now wells up in this family that it almost frightens me. Will it last?

Chapter 31

A New Worry

Maggie

Why are they so against me? I fold the play-school furniture that I assembled earlier and put everything away. It was fun playing teacher even if my students were out of control.

"You're not the boss of me," says David.

"Me neither," chimes Holly, sounding like an echo.

"We're going to the dump and play—so there, teacher."

They drop their pencils and stubbornly walk out. Holly turns to face me and sticks out her tongue. I run after them to call them back, but my pleas fall on deaf ears.

Mom is due home in an hour, and she's the one who put me in charge. She said she'd only be working two days a week for a short period of time, but I just don't know how to make them do what she's asked me to do. I know Mom doesn't like them to play in the dump; it's not really a dump, because no garbage is tossed there, but we call it that. It's two houses west of us where there are many vacant lots far below the sidewalk. During the winter months, children use their sleds or skis to swoop downhill. During the summer a culvert is exposed, and if David and Holly return home stinking so bad that no one can get near them, we know they've been crawling in the sewer pipe. Goodness knows who or what might have been there before them.

I must go after them, so I hurry out the door in the direction of the vacant lots. An hour later, I'm shooing them ahead of me while keeping my distance. Mom is home when we arrive.

"Oh, phew," she says. "Down the basement with both of you and remove your clothes. You two know better than to go into that smelly place. When you're undressed, head for the bathtub."

I go to the back door to throw out the switch I'd picked up for the purpose of getting them home. "I'm sorry, Mom, but they would not mind me even though I told them what you said about my being the responsible one. They will not accept me as someone with the authority you gave me."

"You know why, don't you, Maggie?"

"No."

"It's because you children lived apart for so many years. They think of you as on one side of the fence while they're on the other. It will take time, but we'll get that straightened out. Honey, please go upstairs and run the bath water and see that they get started scrubbing themselves."

I do as I'm told but don't appreciate the treatment I'm given when the two rebellious youngsters finally wiggle into the tub. They usually take separate baths, but tonight there's no other option. I give them soap to share and hand each of them a washcloth as I say, "get busy and scrub," but they continue to ignore me until David makes an ugly face. As I give up and turn to go downstairs, I feel water hit my back.

"Darn you, kids," I holler in exasperation.

When I get to the kitchen and tell Mom what happened, she asks me to have patience. "A good talk will have to come in the near future," she says, "but discipline comes first." "Maggie, take over peeling these potatoes while I go up and get things under control. I doubt they'll be shooting me with water nor will they be doing it to you from now on." She puts down her paring knife and picks up the wooden spoon from the top of the icebox, slaps it on the palm of her hand to make sure it makes a sound as if it smarts, and begins her walk upstairs with each foot landing harder than usual on each step. I know Mom would never use the wooden spoon to slap them, but David and Holly are too young to understand that and won't take any chances.

I moan to myself because it seems like I don't even have a brother and sister. They certainly don't like me, and when they act like this, I don't like them either.

I'll be in the sixth grade this year, and I'll see my old friends again. Until David and Holly treat me more like a sister and not the enemy, I'll have to pretend my friends are my family.

Jenny

"How did your job go today, Jon?" We sit around the small kitchen table where it's a little crowded but cozy. I've prepared bologna and boiled potatoes with peas from the garden. We're all aware the budget is tight so everyone has learned to pitch in and tries to help as much as possible. The garden provides the vegetables, and the children enjoy working there. Jon planted raspberry bushes so I could make wonderful jam, most of which is preserved and tucked away for winter.

"I accomplished a number of stops today," Jon says, "and it was most interesting. The last stop was at the Carlson home, and they'd just finished milking the cows so they gave me a drink of that fresh milk. My gosh, but I haven't tasted anything that good since I was a kid on the farm."

"Did you bring home any of it, Daddy?" David asks. "Is that milk different from what the milkman puts on the back porch every morning?" He helps himself to more peas, puts the bowl down, and once again forgets to pass it on.

"We're not allowed to drink anything that comes right from the cow now because it has to be pasteurized to kill the germs that in this case are called bacteria," Mom explains before she turns to address Daddy. "That was against the law, Jonathan. Did you report it?"

"Good heavens, no, because there's nothing wrong with drinking fresh milk when it comes from cows on a clean farm like the Carlson's. I report what I'm expected to report, nothing like that."

I leave the table to go to the pantry to carry in the saucers filled with gooseberry pudding I made from the berries I picked this afternoon from our bush. I empty the thick cream from the top of the milk bottle and much to the delight of my family put it in a pitcher to serve.

But something lies heavy on my heart this evening, and that's the intense talk I had with Marie today. I barely hear the rest of the conversation at the table.

"Oh, Jenny," she said. "I'm at my wit's end and can no longer find a solution. Carl hasn't worked in months except for a couple odd jobs. My salary won't stretch far enough to make the mortgage payments on Mother's home much longer. If Carl doesn't find work soon we're going to lose the home. We both know that in these tough times there's little hope of selling a house."

It's unusual for Marie to appear distraught, and I don't know what I can do to help. I sense her waiting for my reaction as I wonder what next?

"I see only one solution," Marie says, "and when I ask you this, please give me your thoughts. I've discussed my problem with our sister Ann who says Mother can stay with her for now, but that's only helping one person. Carl might get a WPA or CCC government job except, as I told you before, that isn't happening fast enough to save the house.

"Jenny, I know you've been struggling financially. We could pay you a small amount to help with the rent and light bill if you can find it in your heart to help us. Could we move in with you until Carl finds a job?"

I'm speechless but finally tell her I'd say yes without a second thought, but there's no way I can say yes on my own. I promise to talk to Jonathan as soon as I find him in a good mood.

After I agree to take that step, I know an arrangement like this needs a lot of planning. How do eight of us sleep in a house with three bedrooms and only one bathroom? Who would sleep where? How would we arrange meals and food? A bathroom to prepare for school or work must have assigned times. Where would we keep our individual groceries? We'd have to arrange eating times for each family. My head is spinning.

After a long pause I tell her, "I know you helped me when I needed a home for Maggie. I definitely know that I owe you this, Marie. I'll see what I can do."

But she'll never know how I dread discussing this with Jonathan. They helped Maggie when I needed them, but it doesn't begin to count as much as if they'd helped David or Holly.

Maggie

What a wonderful Christmas we had this year. We went with Mom and Daddy to pick out the tree at a stand in West Duluth. Daddy put it up and hung the lights, and we kids decorated it. It's beautiful. David and Holly didn't like that I wanted them to hang each piece of tinsel separately, so they threw it in bunches when I wasn't looking. I think they were disappointed when I said it was OKAY. Actually, it looked kinda pretty even if I didn't tell them that.

I sit for hours looking at the two little houses and a church we'd been given in Laurel Hill by our parents. My imagination takes off as I pretend I see a small doll walking on the branches to visit every lovely ornament and the village. I hope we can leave the tree up a long time this year. Last year when we were in Auntie and Unkie's cold and drafty house, you could never warm up even when the fireplace was lit. It didn't seem to do much good.

It was special that Daddy's cousin George came to be with us for Christmas. He's so handsome with his wavy hair and mustache, and like Mom says, "I wonder why some pretty lady hasn't snatched him up?" He gave Mom money to buy us kids gifts for Christmas, and I received a pretty yellow cotton dress, my first store-bought dress in years that wasn't a hand-me-down. Mom said it cost three whole dollars.

I also received a fuzzy white bolero that makes me feel special and looks good with the dress. I know the dress is mainly for summer, but I talked Mom into letting me wear it to school after Christmas vacation. I can hardly wait.

Aunt Alma, Uncle Jake, and Grandma were here with us too. Aunt Alma brought a carrot and pineapple salad, my favorite. Grandma prepared the lutefisk Mom bought while

Mom fixed the turkey cousin George sent us a couple days ago. She said there would be lots of leftovers to treat those who visit during Christmas week to see our tree and spend time with us. We had what Mom calls a Norwegian/American supper that was so good!

Daddy isn't feeling well, so he took a nap before we ate. He looks kinda pale and Mom is worried about him.

Chapter 32

Faith, Hope, and Love

Jenny

There's a terrifying crash in the living room, and I rush to see what's happened only to find Jonathan stretched out on the floor. Apparently he has fainted, and as I attempt to help him, I notice a bulging bump on his forehead and see his lower lip is sputtering blood that I continue to dab with my clean hanky.

When he rebounds, he has no clue what happened—knows only that he does not feel well. Jon stayed home from work today because of a fever and pain but evidently was too weak to be up and walking about. I don't hesitate to call our doctor.

It's early evening when Dr. West arrives. After examining Jonathan, he tells me my husband has the flu. He instructs me to give him soup and fluids, and I assure him I will do as he suggests.

Dr. West always diagnoses our family correctly, but this time, he is wrong. A nightmare lasting months follows that fainting episode. It began when Jake and Jonathan's brother Ralph took Jonathan to the hospital. At first the doctors did not know what was wrong until he was diagnosed three days later. They all agree that he has undulant fever.

"What on earth is *undulant fever*?" I ask our doctor. "I've never heard of it."

"Let's sit down, Jenny, and I will try to explain it without getting too technical.

"*Undulant fever* is an infectious disease caused by the bacteria brucella that causes rising and falling fevers, sweats, queasiness, weakness, loss of appetite, headaches, plus muscle and back pain. It's called *undulant fever* because the fever is typically undulant, rising and falling like a wave."

"Oh, Dr. West, that sounds serious."

"I wish I could say it isn't. The incubation period is usually one to three weeks, but sometimes it may be months after exposure.

"He's already had this several weeks, doctor. Does that mean he's now in the several months stage?"

"That's possible, Jenny. It could go on even longer than that. I'm telling you what to expect so this doesn't catch you off guard. If it is a shorter time, I would call it a miracle."

"Could he die, doctor?"

"My dear, let's not even go into that. I'm sure you're aware that anything is possible with a serious disease. He'll be going through a lot of pain and even mental depression. Your role in this won't be easy, so take good care of yourself."

"Is there anything further I need to know in case this goes on for some time?"

"Count your blessings if this doesn't go on for a year or more because then the illness could result in arthritis, chronic fatigue, and even stronger depressive episodes."

I tell myself that I'll count my blessings if he can even hold his job. Right now I feel sick too.

"One thing puzzles me," Dr. West says. "Usually one picks this up from contact with animals or their products. These days, milk is pasteurized, so I don't know how Jonathan could have picked it up from that. Do you have any clue?"

My mind drifts back to a month or two ago when he stopped at some farm and was raving about their fresh milk. "Oh yes, doctor," I tell him. "I do."

A week passes before Jonathan is strong enough to return home from the hospital, and two days later, he's tired of lying in bed and wants to get up. Alma and Jake visit, rejoicing in the good news as we're all sure the fever is now under control. Members of my family come bearing gifts of food. Jon knows it will be some time before he's strong enough to return to work, but he assures everyone he's on his way to better health. Many visitors wish him well.

But time advances, and he doesn't get stronger. The pain returns, and two week later he has a relapse and faints twice while I'm at my part-time job. Maggie finds him when she returns from school. She's relieved when he comes to and helps him into a chair to wait until I get home. I'm very concerned. "Jon," I repeat silently, "this family needs you. You must get well."

A couple days later, his temperature rises to 105 degrees. If I'd been worried before, now I'm unnerved. I rush to my neighbor to call the doctor who tells me to give him aspirin to break the fever and then get back to him. The fever breaks but Jon shakes with chills so powerful our brass bed rattles.

Bless cousin George. He's helped us so many times and is here for us again. He's preparing for a trip to Sweden to see family and friends but stops by with money equaling a month's salary and a car payment so Jonathan can stay home longer. The following Saturday, a delivery man comes with several boxes of groceries. We learn the office spokesman has collected ten cents from each employee in order to purchase boxes of food for us. Included in the gift is a case of newly introduced pop to help Jonathan when he finds it difficult to swallow water. After I pour a glass for him, I let Maggie taste a little, her first. She tells me she didn't know any liquid could be that good.

Jonathan's nerves are now frightfully on edge. Maggie offers to clean the house, so Alma lends us their vacuum cleaner. But Jon can't stand the noise even when she vacuums downstairs and his upstairs bedroom door is shut. I've contacted the Veteran's Hospital in Minneapolis to see if they will accept him there. We're already so in debt to St.

Mary's Hospital here in town that it will take some time to repay them with our small monthly payments.

After a week's wait, Jon gets notice that he's been accepted to the Veteran's Hospital. I joyously rush to his room to tell him the good news. He's barely able to hear my words but manages to say he doesn't want to go. But he'll die if he stays here. He'll need a hospital where he can get the necessary care for as long as he needs it to truly recover. I go to the neighbors and ask to use their phone again; this time to call Alma. She and Jake rush over and sit by Jon's bedside for an hour. When they finally come downstairs, they're extremely drained but have convinced Jonathan to go to Minneapolis.

It's already evening and too late to get ready, but we make arrangements for an ambulance to pick us up tomorrow in time to get Jon on the train for Minneapolis. I will accompany him, and when the locomotive pulls into the big city, another ambulance will be waiting to take us to the Veteran's Hospital in Minneapolis.

Jonathan has now been on what they call "death row" for a week, but doctors finally pull him through. Jon's relatives, in Minneapolis, Richard and Bert, are kind and take me in while I travel on the streetcar to and from the hospital. Now that I'm home again in Duluth, exhaustion smothers me. I've missed the children and am grateful to see them.

I'm also relieved because Jonathan had a change of heart and finally agrees it is okay for Carl, Marie, and Tommy to live with us, *but only until* Carl finds a steady job. He then add, with determination, "Then they're out."

His words don't sting me as much as they could have because I feel certain that as time passes and Jon discovers how helpful and handy Carl is, he will be more lenient. What my husband doesn't appreciate at this time is we actually need Carl when Jon is so ill. There's much work to do around the house that Jon won't be able to do for some time. I'm sure the doctor will insist that he take it easy to gain strength before he returns to work.

Whether Jon's near escape from death will cause his heart to soften towards Marie and her family, I'm not sure. But it means a great deal to me to be able to repay them in some way for their kindness in giving Maggie a home while I was in Milwaukee.

Maggie

Aunt Alma and Unkie drop David and Holly off in my care while they get Mom at the bus depot. I've had such a time with those kids that I can barely wait to discuss this with Mom. She says she'll be down to talk to us as soon as she gets some things out of her suitcase.

She surprises us with souvenirs. Holly gets pink ribbons for her curly blond hair, and David and I get Big Little Books. We both look forward to enjoying them and are grateful. Mine is the story of "It Happened One Night" with pictures of Claudette Colbert and Clark Gable.

After Alma and Jake leave, Mom tells them, "Okay, you two little pumpkins, it's time for bed." I catch her arm and whisper in her ear, "Please let them stay a few minutes longer, Mom. I have something important to talk to you about." She looks puzzled but agrees.

"Sure, honey," she says as she tells the younger ones they can play a little longer before picking up their toys. "Let's go out on the back porch, Maggie. It's a warm evening, and I need some air."

As we settle on the steps and gaze up at a rising full moon, she asks, "What is it, dear?"

"When Auntie and Unkie went to get you at the depot tonight, David and Holly were so sad. Holly even started to cry."

"But why?"

"They were afraid you were going to tell them Daddy died. They were scared we wouldn't have a family anymore and you'd give them to other people to care for them again."

"Oh, Maggie, that isn't good. Thank you for telling me. Please get David and Holly to join us here. Be sure they put on their sweaters. It's beginning to get chilly."

Jenny

The screen door slams behind us, and my children approach with caution.

"Come, children. Let's huddle together and keep warm. I have something to discuss with you." Maggie and David sit on a lower step, and Holly cuddles next to me. They're all so near, and it feels so good. I lock my arms around them.

"There's something I want you to know. If Daddy died, I would never send you out to others to care for you again. We'd still be a family. It might be difficult without Daddy, but we'd make it somehow, but only if we're a united and loving family. We shouldn't have that struggle now as the doctors say that Daddy really will get well this time."

They smile with joy as David says, "Yeah."

"Do you remember when Daddy told us he visited that farm and they gave him some fresh milk? That's what made him sick. Someone told me they are making a movie about Dr. Louis Pasteur. He's the man who discovered the way to pasteurize milk so it would be safe to drink. When I learn when or if the movie is coming, I'll take you all to see it since it has impacted our lives."

David claps. He loves movies.

"Daddy won't drink that milk anymore, will he?" Holly asks. I can sense the fear in her voice.

"You bet he won't, dear. And neither will you knowing how sick it can make anyone who drinks it."

"Now let's talk about Daddy. The doctors say he's getting really well this time, but they must keep him in the Veteran's Hospital in Minneapolis for at least a couple more months until he's strong enough to come home. But we'll get along until then. I'm going to Daddy's office soon to tell them the news. Perhaps there's some work I can do to hold his job until he can go back to work."

"Now I want to discuss how precious family is, so I'm going to ask you some questions. You're the oldest, Maggie, so let's begin with you. Where is your sister?" She points to Holly. "And where is your brother?" She acknowledges David.

"Do you know how wonderful it is to have a brother and sister? Do you know how much they add to a family?"

"I certainly do," Maggie answers.

"And David, where is your sister?" He points to Holly. There's a brief silence before I ask, "Is she your only sister?"

He turns and slowly points to Maggie but says nothing.

"Holly, where is your brother?" No problem.

"And your sister?" That question bothers me. With no one to lead her, I wonder if she'll acknowledge Maggie. She does, and I draw a deep sigh of relief.

"Now I'll ask questions for anyone to answer.

"What does every member of the family need to do to make it a happy and close family?" Silence.

"Do we need to yell at one another?" They all shake their heads.

"Do we need to be kind to one another?" I hear one yes while two of them nod their heads.

It's coming together now. Holly speaks first. She says in a joyful and loud voice. "I know, I know! We need love! My Sunday school teacher taught me that."

David appears as though he doesn't want Holly to direct this discussion, so he's there taking the lead again. *Give him time, Jenny*, I tell myself.

"Daddy needs love, Mama needs love, Holly needs love, and Maggie needs love. And don't forget about David."

We all laugh. "No, David, no one could forget you. Yes, children, you do understand—and I'm proud of you. With everyone working together, giving love and appreciating one another, we can be a terrific family, can't we?"

David says, "You betcha!"

We remain in a huddle perhaps juggling the discussion in our heads. I remember a verse from the Bible and ask my children to listen as I recite it from 1 Corinthians 13:13.

"And now faith, hope, and love abide, these three; and the greatest of these is . . ." I pause. Holly says it first as she smiles with the joy of one who knows the answer.

"It's love, Mama. Love!

The wind is stronger, and I instruct Maggie to take Holly and David upstairs to help them get ready for bed.

"I'll join you soon so we can say our prayers together and exchange good-night kisses."

They do as told, and I lean my head against the building to gaze at the evening sky decorated with twinkling stars and a moon that's now displaying its prominence.

This brings back memories of the last time I was with Paul. For a moment, I stand on the brink of temptation ready to fall into swirling waters before remembering this is but a memory and nothing that I should dwell on. Memories are only good if they make us happy and don't disrupt our lives. If my husband has remembrances, I hope he realizes that.

As much as I cared for Paul, it is now clear that if I had divorced Jon and dated or married Paul, I might have lost my children in the process. The way I see it now, things could never have worked for us. This is the family my children want and need, *but only* if Jonathan and I make the marriage something that is healing for them so we never again hurt our dear ones with such intensity. Maybe it will not be easy, but we can work it out.

Jonathan's words to me when he was so ill in the Minneapolis Veteran's Hospital come back. "Jenny, you are the only woman I've ever really loved." Really loved? I then catch myself again when I realize how petty my thinking is. Whether his expression of love meant that I was the only one, or the one that really mattered, isn't important. He tried, didn't he? Whatever happened in his past, or mine for that matter, should and will no longer be of any consequence if we are to move on to a stronger marriage.

Come, Jenny, I tell myself. *Enough of solving the problems of our future. Show God how much you appreciate His blessings by picking up your weary bones and setting them in the direction of the stairs to join our children with their prayers. Therein, I know, lies my only true happiness.*

THE END

ABOUT THE AUTHOR

A portion of this book is nonfiction, written by an 87-year old woman, who is the 8-year old child "Maggie."

Dorothy Foss lived in Duluth, MN until she married John Simonds and moved to Winona MN where her daughter Pamela was born. They also lived in St. Cloud MN and Superior WI before moving to the Twin Cities in 1960. Her second marriage to Lymon Foss came with a bonus of three stepchildren—Dan, Sue and Jim.

During her employment years, Dorothy worked for CPAs in Duluth, MN, radio station KWNO in Winona, MN, was secretary to the City Manager of Superior, WI, worked for Honeywell, Inc. in Minneapolis, MN for 10 years before being employed by another MN company, Medtronic, Inc. The pacemaker was invented by Earl Bakken, Medtronic's CEO who founded Medtronic, a worldwide pacing company. Dorothy was working for Vice. Pres. Whitney McFarlin when he was appointed to be one of the only two Executive Vice Presidents at the time and reported directly to the President. Dorothy was Mr. McFarlin's Exec. Secy/Admin. Assistant for several years and found this challenge to be the highlight and most enjoyable of her career. She retired from Medtronic after 15 years retaining the personal friendship of numerous great co-workers.

She enjoyed theater with numerous performances in Duluth, Winona, and the Twin Cities. Dorothy studied writing with the Famous Writer's School and the Writer's Digest school for writers. She sold numerous short stories and articles to magazines before turning her creative attention to writing this book.

Edwards Brothers, Inc.
Thorofare, NJ USA
December 5, 2011